BURIAL IN THE CLOUDS

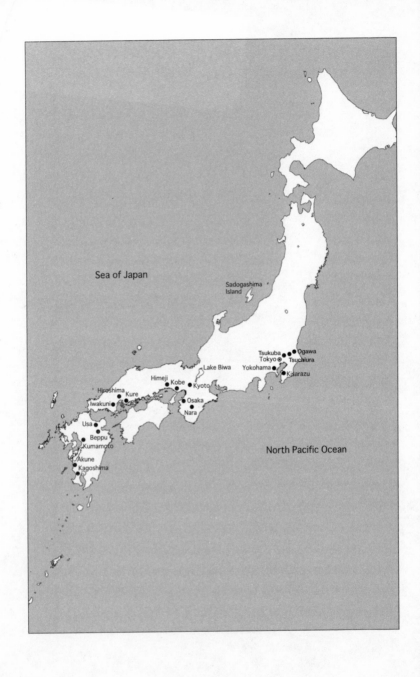

BURIAL IN THE CLOUDS

Hiroyuki Agawa

Translated by Teruyo Shimizu

TUTTLE PUBLISHING
Tokyo • Rutland, Vermont • Singapore

First English-language edition published by Tuttle Publishing, an imprint of Periplus Editions (HK) Ltd., with editorial offices at 364 Innovation Drive, North Clarendon, Vermont 05759 U.S.A.

English translation © 2006 Teruyo Shimizu

"KUMO NO BOHYO" by Hiroyuki Agawa
Copyright © Hiroyuki Agawa 1956.
All rights reserved.

Original Japanese edition published by Shinchosha Co.
This English-language edition published by arrangement with Shinchosha Co., Tokyo, in care of the Tuttle-Mori Agency, Inc., Tokyo.

Library of Congress Cataloging-in-Publication Data
Agawa, Hiroyuki, 1920–
[Kumo no bohyo. English]
Burial in the clouds /Hiroyuki Agawa ; translated by Teruyo Shimizu.—1st ed. p. cm.
ISBN-13: 978-0-8048-3759-0   ISBN-10: 0-8048-3759-7 (pbk.)
I. Shimizu, Teruyo, 1967– II. Title.
PL845.G3K713 2006
895.6'35—dc22
    2006015263

ISBN-10: 0-8048-3759-7
ISBN-13: 978-0-8048-3759-0

Distributed by
North America, Latin America & Europe
Tuttle Publishing
364 Innovation Drive
North Clarendon, VT 05759-9436 U.S.A.
Tel: 1 (802) 773-8930
Fax: 1 (802) 773-6993
info@tuttlepublishing.com
www.tuttlepublishing.com

Asia Pacific
Berkeley Books Pte. Ltd.
130 Joo Seng Road #06-01
Singapore 368357
Tel: (65) 6280-1330
Fax: (65) 6280-6290
inquiries@periplus.com.sg
www.periplus.com

First edition
10 09 08 07 06   10 9 8 7 6 5 4 3 2 1
Printed in Canada

TUTTLE PUBLISHING® is a registered trademark of Tuttle Publishing, a division of Periplus Editions (HK) Ltd.

BURIAL   CLOUDS
     IN THE
       ∽⟳

Otake Naval Barracks (Hiroshima Prefecture)

My first Sunday since joining the Imperial Navy. Our duty today was to organize our belongings. I have recovered my composure somewhat and decided to start this journal.

At 11:50 a.m., the day before yesterday, I stepped off the train at Otake Station and headed for the Naval Barracks. Had a physical exam in the afternoon and passed it as "B" class. I was pronounced flight-worthy, and that determined the course I shall follow. I traded in my school uniform for a sailor's togs (called *jonbira*), and donned that clumsy sailor cap. Our snow-white fatigues were distributed, too. At night, I was taught for the first time how to sling a hammock and how to fold my clothing so as to make a pillow out of it. Had my first navy supper. The dawn following my first night here was cold.

Only four nights have passed since I left bustling Osaka Station, with all my friends and family there to see me off. But I feel now that this must have happened six months ago, a year ago, even three years. It seems like an event lodged deep in the past, and I look back at it as if through the wrong end of a pair of binoculars.

I have no idea whether the navy is hell or paradise, but when I heard the division officer say the word *shaba*—the term navy men use for the "free world" without—I fully realized that I had entered a new realm, utterly different and completely estranged from the snug world I have always inhabited. I knew all of this before, of course. Nevertheless, at one moment my spirit balloons out with a courage that floods my entire body, and I am determined to confront whatever comes. And at the next moment it deflates, and I am vexed and bereft, as if thrown into the abyss. I have a lingering attachment to the studies I left behind. I yearn for my parents. Fond sentiments bind me to so many people. And these feelings twine round and round about me, cutting me to pieces in the end. But I suppose we are no longer to "choose" anything. The only option open to us is to train ourselves, according to a fate already determined.

In the navy a bucket is referred to as a "tin case." A dust cloth is an "inner gunwale match," a tub is a "washtub," and so on. Use of such worldly expressions as *boku, kimi, ne,* and *tono* is absolutely prohibited. One slip of the tongue gets you a "cow killer" from the drill instructor—a disciplinary knuckle on the forehead. I must become proficient at the language and order of this new society. In fact, I need to *master* it, down to the minutest detail.

Scholar-sailors like me are grouped according to the schools we are from. There is the Waseda Division, for example, and the Tokyo University Division. There are Divisions from Chu-o University, from Hiroshima Higher Normal School, and of course from our own Kyoto University. I look about me as I write and see Fujikura, with a long face, chewing his "Jintan" mints. Sakai is writing a postcard. And Kashima—well, he must be someplace around here. In this, I am really quite fortunate.

BURIAL IN THE CLOUDS

After our last seminar on the *Manyoshu*, at the end of November, we played baseball out on the grounds till it grew dark. Then we sat down and talked under a broad oak tree behind the library. Kashima composed a poem for the occasion, which I liked and still remember.

> If I remain in one piece,
> Will there come a time
> When again I see you and you,
> Whom I left under the blue Japanese oak?

It encourages me to no end that half of those old friends are living here together.

The tide of the war is not in our favor, but I don't think it is necessarily in favor of the United States either. I can imagine that American students have given up their study of Shakespeare or Whitman to take their place in the battle line, and in a sense the outcome of the war might well be determined by youths like us. I must sink all impertinent thoughts to the bottom of my mind and try to become a man.

The ceremony officially marking our enlistment is set for Monday, which is tomorrow. The commander-in-chief of the Kure Naval Station will make a tour of inspection. The turn of a vast wheel galvanizes all the merely private movements of our minds, and we are welded, little by little, into a larger organization.

DECEMBER 15

Fujikura was caught reading this morning as the division officer, Lieutenant Yuhara, delivered a moral lecture. The lieutenant defined one aspect of navy spirit as "smartness." He was not talking about stylishness or anything like that. To be "smart," he said, is to be swift, flexible, and agile, all the while retaining a certain grace so as never to be rough. We must acquire this "smartness" in our carriage as well as in our minds, for without it we will be useless to the navy, whether as sailors or as pilots. And then, abruptly, Lieutenant Yuhara thundered:

"Who's that reading? Stand up!"

We all looked on anxiously. The lieutenant demanded to know what Fujikura had in his hands and was baffled when the latter replied that it was a "literary journal." He had to ask again.

"I was reading a literary journal, sir," Fujikura all but shouted, in a tone just a shade defiant. "The article is on Basho, the poet. My old teacher wrote it. I was just thinking that the 'smartness' you describe is rather like the quality Basho has in view when he speaks of his principle of 'lightness.'"

"You mean to tell me that you understood what I said, even while reading?"

"Yes, sir. I did."

We all got a chuckle out of that, except for the division officer himself. "All right," he said. "Put down that magazine and don't let this happen again." He gave no further rebuke. Incidentally, Professor O. wrote that article on Basho, and I remember it with nostalgia. At the same time, I formed no bad impression of Lieutenant Yuhara.

We took the Student Reserve Officers Examination this afternoon. The subjects were Japanese, composition, mathematics, and physics. The proctor was our drill instructor, Petty Officer First Class Zenta Yoshimi. If we pass the exam and finish our course at the naval barracks, in a little more than a month we will be given a naval officer's uniform and assigned a rank just below midshipman, and we will start acquiring skills specific to our positions. I'll probably be sent to the Tsuchiura Naval Air Station.

Petty Officer Yoshimi is among the surviving crew of the aircraft carrier *So-ryu*, which was sunk at the Battle of Midway Island. He is a veteran of ten years' standing, yet before long we will outrank him. And if we find ourselves together on the same battlefield, we students must assume command, taking into our hands the lives of officers like these. We cannot treat the matter lightly. I can well imagine that it won't be pleasant for these drill instructors to see students like us—men who don't know their left from their right—outrank them, and in such short order, too. But at least our instructor, Petty Officer Yoshimi, has the good humor to say, with a laugh, that he "has now become a college professor." Besides, he takes his responsibilities seriously and never makes unreasonable demands of us.

As for the examinations: It is a piece of cake for us to tackle Japanese and composition, but we humanities students are totally out of our element in mathematics and physics. I have only the faintest memory of ever hearing such terms as "Ohm's law," or Helmholtz's "Conservation of Energy," and *that* was when I was in junior high school. Everybody is having trouble. However, navy custom fosters a decidedly strong rivalry among its various divisions and outfits, and to that rule the Student Reserve Officers Exam is no exception. The drill instructors would do anything to avoid the dishonor of producing a failure from their own outfits. So the proctors themselves cheat. Petty Officer Yoshimi paused once beside my desk and rapped it with a pencil. I turned, but he stepped away as if nothing had happened. Whereupon I scrutinized the paper: I had given the wrong answer to one of the questions in mathematics. I looked around me and saw our proctor rapping, here and there, as he walked among the desks.

In the evening, we had a special course in navy calisthenics.

DECEMBER 28

Our third time rowing the cutter. About fifty strokes. I can think of nothing more beautiful and orderly to look at, and yet more arduous to do myself. But I have to pull my own weight.

Navy mottoes: Iron will. Order. Initiative. And above all, *praxis*.

But honestly, I know my heart always harbors the antitheses of all these elements of virtue, side by side with each of them. Weakness. Slovenliness. Passive maintenance of the status quo. And above all, just going through the motions. As for that last one: I'm really not shrewd enough to pull it off, though I sometimes feel that you *have* to pull it off if you want to survive in the military.

"*Ingenuity*, Yoshino," Fujikura said to me bluntly during a cigarette break. "*Ingenuity*. I tell you this because you're rather naively honest. We can do what we're asked to do without letting ourselves be cast into the mold of this insular navy world. If you can't salvage at least that much independence, to what purpose have you lived such a free and easy life at high school and university? Of course, the brass would be furious if we didn't at least *appear* to fit their mold, and that's where the ingenuity comes in. You know, the novelist Ryunosuke Akutagawa once said, 'There is also a truth that can only be told through lies.'"

Fujikura still won't use military talk like *kisama, ore,* and *omae,** unless a supervisor is within earshot. He seems to enjoy putting up a little resistance. I don't always agree with him, but I can listen to anything with an open mind so long as it comes from Kashima or Fujikura. Among the four of us, it's Fujikura and Kashima who rebel most strongly against the navy atmosphere. Sakai is the most amenable, though he's timid and somewhat whiny. And I'd say I'm just about in between.

The navy adheres to a diet of brown rice, and before each meal a voice bellows instructions from the loudspeakers. *Dinner is ready! Wash your hands! Chew thoroughly and eat slowly! Chew thoroughly and eat slowly!*

We always heard that in the military you have to eat quickly, or else they teach you a lesson. To prepare ourselves we even staged an eating contest at a restaurant we used to haunt called Ogawa-tei, if only for fun. But I find that in the navy it's actually the other way round. I don't know whether this has anything to do with it, but the sailors, to a man, empty their bowels with remarkable frequency, quite as if their bodies had somehow altered. I myself take a good hard shit three times a day, every day. The bathroom is always packed during short breaks. If you delay getting in line, you miss your chance. It's quite painful to engage in battle drills while holding at bay so urgent a call of nature. This is especially true when you have to stand at attention. Your lower abdomen feels bloated, and you have to struggle not

---

**Kisama, ore,* and *omae* mean, respectively, "you," "I," and, again "you." They have a rugged, masculine sound in Japanese and would be more commonly used among soldiers, sailors, and so on. (In Japanese there are a number of equivalents for any given English personal pronoun; their usage can vary according to gender, degree of formality, and so on.)

to let out a fart. Maybe I should get up in the middle of the night and finish off a portion of the business. That might be an example of "ingenuity."

A new year begins. Our first march to Iwakuni. For the first time since joining the navy, I breathed the air of the outside world. Chickens clucking. Children playing battledore and shuttlecock in their Sunday best. A drunk peddler taking a leak by the road, his bicycle at his side. The sights and sounds of the holiday impressed me vividly. The waters of the Iwakuni River ran clear, with round, white pebbles covering the bottom. The landscape around the Kintaikyo Bridge reminded me of the country near Togetsukyo Bridge in Arashiyama, in the western suburbs of Kyoto. We returned to base in the evening.

I want something sweet. For two weeks I have been craving *botamochi*. What preoccupies me most since I entered the navy? Well, I find myself always thinking of food. I don't have any sexual desire at all, probably because I haven't had any experience, but I certainly desire *mame-daifuku*, beautifully browned over red-hot charcoal. Just one more time I want to sit down to some breaded pork cutlets at Ogawa-tei.

We are eating white rice for the first three days of the New Year. I am so used to staring at brown rice day after day that freshly cooked white rice, with its moist, pearly finish, is precious in my sight. Lunch was served at 1000 on New Year's Day: salad, steamed fish cake, herring roe, sweet black beans, beef, and soft azuki-bean jelly, immediately followed by two parcels of treats, an apple, and four satsuma oranges. We were told, however, that we had to polish it all off at the table. We were forbidden to set anything aside for later. We wondered why, but as they say, we haven't mastered soldiering yet if we are forever asking why. Nobody openly opposes that idea, and yet isn't it true that skepticism is the father of modern science? And isn't the navy, above all, founded upon the modern science of the West? I mean, the navy is hardly the infantry. Naval officers know perfectly well that soldiership alone can't move its warships and aircraft. Isn't this all something of a paradox?

Anyway, it seems that if you wish for something from the bottom of your heart, you will be heard. Last night, unbeknownst to me, someone laid three dried persimmons in my hammock. And there was another anonymous gift today of five miso-seasoned rice crackers. It requires supreme skill to eat rice crackers without making any noise. They say that, even now, with the world cut in two by the war, there are ways to get steel from Sweden or equipment from the United States, if you only have the will to do it. And in much the same way, we aren't shut off completely from the outer world. For example, the father of S. in my outfit is a man of some influence in the city of Otake, and he manages to send food in through the executive officer at the naval barracks. This accounts for the miso-seasoned rice crackers, a bequest from S.

Kashima belongs to the outfit bunking next to us. As New Year's Eve wound to a close, he was startled by a sharp, goblin-like cackle, coming at him from above: "Hey, Kashima! Kashima!" Before he could recover from the shock, he was hauled up onto a broom closet. There, with Drill Instructor Ishii at his side, Kashima found himself forced to wolf down dried persimmons and twenty-odd boiled eggs. The story goes that Kashima's father came for a visit bearing various morsels for him to eat during the New Year holiday. However, he was not allowed to see his son. "Well, it's a shame to waste this," he said. "Please share it with the instructors." And he left all the food for them. Many fathers and mothers reportedly come out to visit their sons only to be turned away. Some try to bribe their way in, and the drill instructors have been known to wink at the practice. I don't like this sort of business, but I could sell my soul when it comes to food. Needless to say, last night's dried persimmons came from Kashima.

During study session New Year's Eve, a fellow got caught drawing elaborate pictures of an *oyako-donburi*, curried rice, and all manner of cakes. This was M., of the 6th outfit, and he used pencils in twelve different colors to sketch these painstakingly detailed pictures. But no matter, they ended up torn to bits. He received a slap on each cheek from the division officer. Fortunately, I have yet to suffer a blow since joining the navy.

JANUARY 7

The cold last night chilled me to the bone, and, sure enough, we had snow this morning. It has been falling steadily ever since, blanketing the mountains of the Chugoku district and the islands of the Seto Inland Sea.

Bending and stretching exercises. Jogging. Then rowing drills in the cutter.

"Make it snappy! Go!" Petty Officer Yoshimi barked out his commands, banging on the broadside. But that was just while we were boarding the boat, and with the division officer overseeing the exercise. Once we were out in the offing, he ordered us to cross oars, and then he gave us a little talk. We snuggled up together to get warm, like a group of chicks, and rubbed our hands as we listened. Itsuku-shima Island, which before had always looked blackish-blue, lay powdered in the snowy inland sea. A thin layer of snow covered the cutter, too. I could make out two German submarines in port.

Petty Officer Yoshimi told us the story of how his warship, the *So-ryu*, went down at Midway Island. That battle was a watershed defeat for Japan, and we have now lost nearly all our big carriers: the *Akagi*, the *Kaga*, the *Ryu-jo*, the *So-ryu*, the *Hi-ryu*, and the *Sho-ho*. The auxiliary aircraft carrier *Chu-yo* was also sunk recently. According to the officer, the *Chu-yo* used to be a Japanese mail-boat called the *Nitta-maru*, but it was converted into a warship. Only two vessels, the *Shokaku* and the *Zuikaku*, remain in service as purpose-built aircraft carriers. From now on, he explained, the war will be an extremely difficult affair for Japan. He doesn't think our prospects are necessarily as bright as the radio reports from Imperial Headquarters suggest. The men who have taken part in actual combat know this better than anybody else. All of us, he added, should understand that our lives will likely end sometime next spring; we must prepare. Officer Yoshimi spoke with feeling, and his words absorbed us utterly. We forgot even to rub our hands. Before long, he also said, we will join operational units as officers, and our sense of responsibility might well lead us to impose severe discipline on our subordinates. The more earnest and dedicated we are, he suggested, the more we will be prone to do that, but the fact is that there are many occasions when neither the character nor the degree of the discipline we enforce has any bearing at all on the wider situation. It is perfectly all right to tighten the reins, to push the men, or even to beat them if necessary. However, Officer Yoshimi said that he wants us all to take care to discern *when* to come down hard, and also to slacken up a little bit, occasionally turning a blind eye to the men. How gratifying that is for deprived young soldiers! He urged us never to forget how we felt during our brief period as seaman recruits at the naval barracks.

Later, a man in my outfit criticized Petty Officer Yoshimi. He claimed this little speech was done from calculation, that Officer Yoshimi says we'll all be dead next spring, but all the while is just shrewdly looking out for his own hide in a way perfectly characteristic of petty officers. Well, I can't agree, and it is impertinent of that fellow to say such a thing, pulling a rank he doesn't even have yet. If we indulge ourselves in *needless* conceit and lose our humility, we will surely invite *needless* troubles.

It's so cold that my fingers are almost numb, but I'm getting the hang of rowing the cutter. Also we are learning light signals, semaphore, and rope work. Rope work involves the half hitch, two half hitch, bowline knot, bowline on the bight, sheet bend, log hitch, and so on, and is all rather complicated. We learn to clean the toilet and do the laundry, how to wash socks as well. It seems I'm gradually assimilating myself to navy life. They say we'll leave this barracks on the 25th of this month at the latest.

We had hot tofu miso soup and a sardine for dinner. The fish, complete with its head and tail, had plenty of fat, and the saltiness penetrated it. Quite good. I saw a guy slip a second sardine into his bowl of rice, taking advantage of its being his turn to serve the meal. He hid the fish well, but inevitably it poked its head out as he ate. Still he kept at it, cool as a cucumber. Is this what we should expect of someone from the law college at Kyoto University? His conduct is beneath contempt, but all the same I clearly envy him that one sardine—intensely. Why do I get so hungry?

Quite unexpectedly, we will be allowed to have visitors on the 14th. I sent out a mimeographed invitation today, and asked for *A Trip to Manyo* by Bunmei Tsuchiya, *The Complete Works of Sakutaro Hagiwara*, matches, mentholatum, and medicine for stomachaches.

Another secret gift of sweets tonight: *an-mochi*. As I munched mine in the hammock, I thought of seeing my parents, and I was thrilled.

JANUARY 10

A cluster of letters has arrived from Professors O. and E. at Kyoto University, from my old high school teacher Mr. N., and so on. Kashima, Sakai, Fujikura, and I sat around the cigarette tray during the break, exchanging postcards. It has been quite a while since we had so lively a discussion of the *Manyoshu* and the scenery and customs of Yamato (the very heart of the anthology). But as we talked I noticed a certain look on the face of a fellow from another division, and it struck me that we should take care lest our most innocent conversation sound strangely pedantic. This is the case even in a company of seamen with an academic background, and soon enough we'll be assigned to operational units, where we must mingle with career officers and enlisted men. We really can't indulge this pointless nostalgia for university life. We should tuck it away deep in our hearts until the world is again at peace—that is, if we survive the war.

All the same, I enjoyed the conversation. What a consolation it was to chat about the three mountains of Yamato, about Mt. Futakami, the Yamanobe Pass, the streaming Furukawa River, and about all the places we visited during our *Manyo* trip last winter! In the town of Nabari, we played the card game *karuta* at an inn, warming ourselves in a *kotatsu* built into the floor, while out back brown-eared bulbuls swooped down from the hill to eat the red berries of the oleaster. I also remember sitting up through the night once, at the inner temple of Nigatsu-do, for the water-drawing ceremony spoken of in Basho's poem.

> The water-drawing ceremony:
> Footsteps of the priest
> Who confines himself in the temple for prayer.

When midwinter ends, the water-drawing season will come again to Nara. I distinctly remember how my feet felt as I tread on the thin ice, and as muddy water seeped into my worn-out shoes. After all, we entrusted our very lives to these "things of Yamato" and to the *Manyoshu*. But I have to remember: All that is just a fine memory now, a lovely bit of atmosphere, and this isn't the time to dwell on an atmosphere. War is about to teach me firsthand what the poet Otomo no Tabito felt when he was sent to fill a government post at Dazaifu, that remote land where "incessantly the light snow falls," as he once put it. So I will set aside my studies for the moment and devote myself utterly to the navy. This can only deepen my understanding of the *Manyo* poems anyway, should I be fortunate enough to outlive the war. I really have to believe that.

Mr. N. reports in his letter that he will be participating in "rites of purification" and other such things at the Training Center for Doctrine in Koganei-cho, Kita-tama, Tokyo, through February 9. I hardly know what to think about that. He says each high school is to send one teacher to study these rites, but I have to wonder: Could this sort of thing possibly help usher in a new era? Is it really worth the bother? Or is it just useless folly, like rowing against the current? If you ask me, instead of abandoning their vocation for "rites of purification," I would much prefer that teachers and students put their hearts into their studies just as they did before the war—no, even *more* diligently than they did before the war, so as to make up for our absence. I hear that the professors' offices at the university are all desolate. Letters trail in to them, one by one, from students who joined the army and wound up in some transport unit in Fushimi, in some regiment in Takahata, Nara, or in scattered places such as Kagoshima, Tokyo, or Manchuria.

JANUARY 12

Well, it happened, exactly as I feared it would. Some student in the 217th Division got off a wisecrack. "You see," he said to a drill instructor decorated with four good conduct medals—to the guardian spirit of the navy, so to speak—"You see, I'll take good care of you when I receive my commission. So why don't we meet each other halfway? You know, give-and-take." As a result, everyone in the 217th was ordered this evening to do push-ups with their feet up on chairs, almost in the position of a handstand. And while they were at it, they got a good "dive-bombing" in the bargain (that's when an officer gathers all his momentum and thrashes you on the ass). Next, they were doused with cold water from the washtub. Their strength was utterly depleted. Men whose brittle arms could no longer support the weight of their bodies were forced to lick the water off the deck. My heart ached when I heard how severe this correction was, but I'd better not quail at it. They say that in the army much worse punishments (and far more unreasonable ones, too) are a matter of course. I can't pamper myself or give in to conceit. I must come to grips with the realities of military life. This incident happened in another division, but I have to learn from it nonetheless.

Smoking alone at night, I gazed up at Sirius, its bright light flaring off the lower left side of Orion.

JANUARY 14

Today, a series of military reviews.

Received visitors after that. Father and mother came to see me. My father said the train was so packed that they had to stand all the way from Osaka. Mother had sunken eyes. The two hours given to us, from twelve to fourteen hundred hours, passed all too quickly. I forgot myself, and now I have no clear memory either of what I heard or what I said. It seems I just repeated such commonplaces as "I'm all right," "I'm trying my best," or "I don't find things so difficult," all the while feeling embarrassed as my mother gazed at me in my sailor suit, half in admiration, half in pity. My parents told me that my brother Bunkichi has been transferred to a newly organized unit that set out from the port of Osaka on the 8th. He is now a corporal. Still, he was allowed to spend some four hours at home before departing. "Today may be the last time I see you in this life," he told our parents, looking very sad. As he was wearing a summer outfit, my parents speculate that he will be sent to some island in the Pacific. I don't worry so much about my own situation, but I really am anxious when it comes to my brother. He is timid, has a weak constitution, and was drafted at the age of thirty-four. My mother grumbled that she didn't know who would inherit the family business. "Don't bring up an issue like that," I chided her. "How could I possibly make an answer now?" Nevertheless, I grew quite emotional when I heard that Professor E. said to them, "Please tell him to take good care of himself," and also when my father said, "We'll come see you anywhere, whenever they allow us a meeting."

The reception room is located to the right of the gate to the naval barracks. It was a lovely day, sunny and warm, and it made me wistful to think that we were forbidden to eat anything. I saw many a regretful face scattered about, gazing at what must have been big bundles of *botamochi*, or sushi, or red rice. "Father and I can cover for you. No one will see. Why don't you try some?" said one young mother, almost pleading. Her eyes misted up when her son replied in a whisper, but still maintaining his military bearing, "No, it is not permitted." Filial devotion is a blessing, but it can also be ticklish, and in our case that devotion might well turn out to be a burden at times.

Anyway, what ingenuity Fujikura possesses! When the meeting ended, his gaiters were all puffed out and gawky. And after the inspection, two satsuma oranges materialized in my hammock. I felt guilty indulging my appetite when my friend had borne all the risk (I never got *my* hands dirty). But I accepted the gift with gratitude.

The commander of the naval barracks has changed. Rear admiral Takaaki Kamai just arrived to fill the post. We saw off his predecessor, waving our caps.

There was a dress inspection this afternoon, followed by the drills in which we sling and fold up our hammocks as quickly as possible. Very tough.

About a week ago, I wrote in this diary that devoting myself entirely to the navy would only deepen my appreciation of literature, should I survive the war. Then it occurred to me that this way of thinking—that is, treating navy life as a means to a strictly private end—not only contradicts the idea of "devoting myself to the navy," it also suggests that I am anything but prepared to endure an ordeal that will carry us beyond our physical and mental limits. At the end of the day, when I take a hard, honest look at myself, I see how desperately I wish to live through the war and return to private life. It horrifies me to call to mind what Officer Yoshimi told us in the cutter on that snowy day a while ago. I loved the literary vocation to which I had aspired, loved it completely. Good friends, good professors, tranquil offices, and beautiful poems. No doubt it had its sentimental side, but I studied with all my heart. I sowed and watered the soil, and I have harvested nothing yet. I can't bear to think that I may close my life of twenty-three years and several months without harvesting a single crop in what I believed to be my true calling. Perhaps I just lack the good grace to give it all up.

Yesterday we ran races in full battle gear, then had a tea party in the afternoon. After the tea, the results of the Student Reserve Officers Examinations were announced, and, as I expected, I have been assigned to the aviation branch, and will be sent to the Tsuchiura Naval Air Station in Ibaraki Prefecture. It never occurred to me a year ago that I would become a navy flyer.

Law graduates like Yonemura and Yoshizawa will go to the Naval Paymaster's College in Tukiji, Tokyo. Kashima has been assigned to the seaman branch and will head for Takeyama Naval Barracks in Yokosuka, Kanagawa. My Tsuchiura group is to be the last to depart, so we spent a busy afternoon packing lunches for Kashima and his fellow seamen. The bamboo husks we used to wrap the food in were small, but we had no good alternative. Anyhow, we kept struggling at the task. We took the greatest possible care we could, out of respect.

At one-forty, in the middle of the night, the Yokosuka group folded their hammocks and left the barracks en masse. Will the day come, I wondered, when we meet again under that blue oak tree, as Kashima said in his poem, given that we can't assume we shall live even to see tomorrow? Following navy custom, we simply raised our hands in salute and waved our caps, without shaking hands or patting each other on the shoulders. A lump rose in my throat, but with no opportunity to speak to Kashima, I just continuously saw the men off as they marched in their long line across the dark wintry grounds, all in their identical seaman's uniform. With some of these men, I had kicked a ball about on the field, sung, and debated philosophy, until just two months ago. I will probably never see them again.

Kashima is rather bohemian. He acquainted himself once with the proprietress of a certain "tea house" in Miyagawa-cho. He hung out there all the time—all but boarded there. On another occasion he simply cut his classes and military drills, sojourning for a month at a hot spring in Aomori. Like Fujikura, he has been either harshly critical of the war, or else indifferent to it. But now I suppose he, too, has but one choice—namely, to bear his fate with courage, and fight battles. I wanted to say a word of farewell to thank him for the dried persimmons, but it was too dark for me to make him out in the long procession.

Fujikura and Sakai have also been assigned to the aviation branch. That means they will go to Tsuchiura with me. After the Yokosuka group left, the long row of hammocks looked like a set of gums with teeth missing. It was ominous. We were given travel expenses and briefed on the journey in the afternoon. We set forth tomorrow morning.

Tsuchiura Naval Air Station

FEBRUARY 20

It's Sunday, but it looks like we won't be allowed to leave the base for a while.

The chief instructor gave us a sermon after morning assembly. He said the reputation of student reservists like us is absolutely rotten, not merely in each operational unit, but at headquarters too. Our general slipshoddiness, he said, and our deficiencies as to loyalty, have drawn severe fire within the military establishment. Some even ventured to suggest that we student reservists are little better than monkeys dolled up in officers' uniforms. So he wondered: Had we ever really made up our minds to devote ourselves to the navy? Didn't some of us still regard navy life as a kind of interim arrangement? We should never entertain thoughts of visiting home, not even if our parents die. Each one of us shall perish in the decisive engagements of the war by this coming summer. Continue to be off guard, he admonished, and we would sully the tradition of the Imperial Navy. If we should ever find ourselves of two minds, suspended between the possibilities of life and death, we should without hesitation choose death. Etc. etc.

It's not that we must prepare ourselves to die by summer. No, he is telling us simply *to die.* They never miss an opportunity to tell us to die. What, in the name of heaven, is their goal? Is it to carry the war through to completion, or merely to kill us all? If we really can save our country by dying, then by all means let us do precisely that. Since February 1, the day of the ceremony marking the assignment of the 14th Class of student reserves to the aviation branch, we have known that we must confront death. We are trying hard, lame though we may be, to brace ourselves for it, yet I cannot for the life of me believe that dying is *itself* the goal. It is pointless, no matter how you look at it, to rush headlong and heedless into the grave, and if I follow the chief instructor's dictates to the letter, wouldn't it qualify as "disloyalty" even to seek shelter during an air raid? I'm not a rebel like Fujikura, but even I took offense at the chief instructor's words. After all, who made us give up our academic work? Who rounded up these "monkeys" and put them in uniform?

Our life at Tsuchiura Naval Air Station is simply inhumane. Cigarettes are strictly rationed. Not because we don't have a sufficient supply, it is just that we should not in any degree be comfortable. So I seldom smoke, and when I smoke I feel dizzy.

As for correspondence, we are permitted only one postcard a week. But then the one postcard I wrote last week, to Kashima at Takeyama Naval Barracks, was returned to me because the censor said my handwriting was too small! I was instructed to write in a large hand, with characters the size of my thumb. I'd like to believe that all this bother actually contributes to my training. Anyway, I've grown used to treating a postcard on my desk as a treasure, and to debating whom I should send that treasure to each week until I'm quite at a loss, and I can't say that there isn't a kind of condensed pleasure in all this. Still, I don't want to be such easy game as to consider it a meaningful exercise to sum up in just four lines of stamp-sized characters what is overflowing in my mind.

I told Fujikura that I think this war has historical significance, that, to say the least, Japan is obviously in a fateful crisis, that we do wish to give our all to save her, but that I can't countenance entrusting our lives wholesale to a bunch of hysterical, fat-headed career officers—to men who regard us as monkeys undermined by "liberal education." Fujikura said it is all too late. He opposes war on general principles, but he has always felt that there is something fundamentally wrong with *this* war in particular. He can't say what exactly, but of this much he is certain: The war is essentially an extension of the so-called China Incident.* And what about the China Incident? As a matter of fact, he has given much thought to the matter, and cannot conclude, no matter how he looks at it, that justice was on our side. Japan should not have fought to begin with. We should have sought to settle the China Incident in such a way as to save face on both sides. Anyway, he said, that is all water under the bridge now. He may be destined to die before long, and there is nothing he can do. But, he added, not once has he ever wished to offer up his every effort, as I do. I'd very much like to discuss all this further with Fujikura if the opportunity arises. Strange to say, I noticed that, somewhere along the way, even he has ceased to use worldly terms like *kimi* and *boku*.†

    We cleaned our quarters in the morning.

    Those who needed a haircut visited the barber's next to the canteen after the cleanup. It takes two minutes per head and costs fifteen sen. It's certainly cheap, but what's more amazing is the speed. The barber's clipper makes three or four round trips on the scalp, and it's done. We all ran back, with bits of soapy foam clinging to our ears. Then we had our pictures taken, one group at a time. We posed with our caps, on which our names had been chalked, in front of our chests. Our heads were all shiny, and we looked just like a group of convicts.

---

* The China Incident is a reference to the fighting between Japanese forces and nationalist Chinese forces in July of 1937 at the Marco Polo Bridge (near Beijing), which sparked the Sino-Japanese War (1937–45).

† These words all have either slightly feminine or informal connotations, hence their disuse in military contexts. *Boku* is a first-person pronoun ("I"); *kimi*, a second-person pronoun ("you"); *ne* is in this context roughly equivalent to "to be"; *tono*, a suffix sometimes applied to names as an honorific.

Sang martial songs from 1600, including "Lord Kusunoki and His Son," "Death Squad," and "The Brave Fight of the Akagi." The sun was setting, and as we sang, marching around the drill ground in double loops, I was moved by the sheer vitality that young men like us possess.

Took a bath after dinner. It was a nice hot bath, and I had a good stretch for the first time in what seems like years. I emptied my bowels twice during the night. And thus my Sunday wound to a close.

FEBRUARY 22

On the 17th and 18th an enemy task force attacked the Truk Islands, and today's papers reveal the results. We lost two cruisers, three destroyers, thirteen transport vessels, and one hundred twenty aircraft. The sinking of a single ship is major news in times of peace, and detailed accounts of the incident and any number of harrowing stories fill the pages of the newspapers. But all I see in front of me today is a set of cold figures, bluntly presented. For our part, we have learned, over time, to look at the figures alone, and to give no thought to the brutal realities that have unfolded behind them.

In the special course, we played interdivisional games of "Capture the Pole." Our opponent was the 7th Division. "Capture the Pole" is a fierce game in which you are permitted to punch, to kick, and even to die. (Honestly, there *was* a casualty at this station last year.) "How can we imitate the boys at the Naval Academy?" some of the fellows grumbled. It is all so silly. Still, they formed their line, stripped to the waist and going barefoot. And once the whistle sounded, most got fired up like fighting dogs. Only after the fact did I reflect on the combative instinct in men.

I was in the attacking party. As I gathered momentum and thrust myself forward, I noticed Sakai in the 7th Division. He kept up a constant battle cry through the top of his head, as he stayed busily engaged for the sake of appearance, dashing about, this way and that, dodging skillfully. A wave of real antagonism rose in me, and I pounced on him. He slipped away, and soon I found myself drawn into a vortex of friends and foes. In no time, my head was forced down by a forest of wobbling legs in white fatigues. I was beaten, kicked, and trampled, countless times. I endured it all, seeing stars often enough, surely. Then the whistle sounded again, and our victory was confirmed. It was rather exhilarating to win, as I found out. Sakai approached me later, wearing an annoyed expression. He said he never dreamt I would rush him with such a ferocious look, even granting the fact that we were opponents.

The word is that the division officers of some of the defeated teams were so out of humor that they canceled dinner. Speaking of which, we had beef stew tonight. It contained a surprisingly generous amount of meat that had been steeped in sauce, though the latter was a bit on the floury side. Uncommonly delicious. Other defeated divisions found themselves slapped with sanctions, too, a snack withheld here, cigarettes denied there. On the other hand, I hear that one of the other winning divisions was allowed an extra postcard.

After the study session, we recited the "Five Reflections." I heard that we must do this every night before taking down the hammocks. We are to straighten up and close our eyes, and as the student on duty softly reads out each item, we (supposedly) reflect, solemnly, on the events of the day.

–Hast thou not gone against sincerity?
–Hast thou not felt ashamed of thy words and deeds?
–Hast thou not lacked vigor?
–Hast thou exerted all possible efforts?
–Hast thou not become slothful?

N. poked my knee and whispered. "Doesn't 'Hast thou not become slothful?' sound ridiculous somehow?" I almost burst into laughter, but managed to hold it back. It would have been a disaster if I hadn't. In any case, they impose on us, at every opportunity, what is in fact a kind of mockery of the education the men receive at the Naval Academy in Eta-jima, which only feeds the antipathy of the students here. Even I am bothered by it. Much more so after seeing a captain, a full-fledged graduate of the Naval Academy, have parcels of pond smelt from Lake Kasumiga-ura shipped home on official flights. Our minds are not necessarily simple. For example, this diary differs altogether from the "Cadet Journal" I submit to the division officer, and which I am obliged to keep (again, in imitation of the practices at Eta-jima). In the journal meant for his eyes, my spirit already approaches the level of a war god.

FEBRUARY 26

I experienced sexual urges practically for the first time since joining the navy. I was in some kind of trance, clasping a woman's warm hand in mine, and listening to a melody on the thirteen-stringed *koto*. (This all happened in a dream.) The woman wasn't anyone I knew, and I couldn't see her face. It was just a woman's warm, meltingly supple hand. A fat goldfish swam leisurely around our two clasped hands, trailing algae behind it. As for the tune I heard on the *koto,* "The Dance of the Cherry Blossoms": that turned up in the dream because the Yokosuka military band came yesterday and performed it. I don't feel like saying anything more. It was a wet dream.

Many of the men exchange dirty quips, but few, I gather, actually suffer from frustrated sexual desires. It was an unusual incident for me.

MARCH 1

The weather here is highly changeable. Strong winds blow, kicking up huge clouds of dust, into which Mt. Tsukuba disappears. The surface of Lake Kasumiga-ura itself gets dusty from time to time. They say this heralds the coming of spring, but however that may be, the weather is certainly fierce here, as the anonymous poem in the *Manyoshu* suggests: "the leaves in Musashino bend to and fro before the wind. . . ." It is hard for Kansai people to get used to. Today, on the other hand, was actually quite warm. Energetic young trainee pilots tumbled through the wind in those big steel hoops. At night, when we get a break from our studies, we hear what might well be taken for the howling of dogs, as the trainees rehearse their shrill commands. They bed down soon afterwards, and I wonder if they dream the dreams of childhood. Something about their voices, and the way they look, puts me in mind of those *Manyoshu* poems by the *sakimori*—the young soldiers garrisoned in Kyushu in ancient days, so young as to still be smelling of milk. It gives me a catch in the throat.

As for our own group, today we were ordered to toss our jackets into the ditch below Waka-washi Bridge. Why? Because we left them in a pile during morning calisthenics. One by one, we were made to throw our white jackets into a filthy stream near Lake Kasumiga-ura, and then made to fetch them out again. This is too sadistic, too absurd. At night, we were all smacked in the face because we failed to fold our blankets properly. That was the eighth blow I've taken since arriving at Tsuchiura. A deck officer did the work. He knew that his hand would be badly swollen after slapping four hundred twenty men in the face, so he ordered the student assistant on duty to bring a washtub of water for him to cool his fist in as he carried out the task. Judging from the pitying look on his face, the student assistant obviously thought he would be exempted, but he also got his in the end.

We are watched every minute of the day. Maybe it isn't easy to be the deck officer who constantly picks at us, but neither is it easy to live under such relentless surveillance. I realize I have been looking forward to emptying my bowels recently. The toilet is just about the only place where we really can lock ourselves in. There, I relish complete solitude, at least for five minutes.

A false rumor is making the rounds. The word is we are to leave this naval air station at the end of March, possibly to be posted overseas for flight training. *Let's go! Let's do it!*, I said to myself. *Let's really become pilots!* To be sure, my mind suffers its contradictions, endlessly vacillating this way and that, but when the time comes, I will die bravely. Our life at this base is just too tiresome.

Lately we have done nothing but practice Morse code, day in and day out. We got bad marks again today. The average score for the division was 81.7, and we were denied our snack as a result. It's contemptible of them to manipulate our physical desires every chance they get, simply to make us work harder. I myself missed three letters today. The *ki* sound is represented as — · — · ·", which corresponds to "*kii te hoo ko ku*" (or, "listen and report?) in our mnemonics. But Fujikura routinely makes us chuckle by mocking the pattern with "*kii te hoo ko ku, mi te jigoku*" (or, "listen and report; you see it and it's hell"). Consequently, I mistook *ki* for *mi*, and by the time I noticed the error I had already missed three letters.

MARCH 8

It was overcast today. The wind shifted from south to east. The sun peeked out now and then, making it feel like spring. I saw some odd-looking sailboats on Lake Kasumiga-ura, and fresh grass on the opposite bank. In the center of the drill ground four gliders stood neatly arrayed, their wings in alignment.

Our morning lesson was glider training. Once every sixteen turns, I would cry out, "Cadet Yoshino, #39, ground run start," and then taxi the glider for about twenty seconds. That's it for now, but the pleasant shock of it all makes me feel as if we really are taking our first steps skyward. In flight lessons the other day, we were allowed to climb into a Junker and, for the first time, get our hands on the control stick. It thrills me to think we are about to tread a path into the clouds. No doubt it is also the path to the grave, but that doesn't get me down. What's depressing and annoying are all the daily trivialities.

I was running back from the bath, soap case in my right hand, washcloth in my left, when I came across the assistant division officer. I was bewildered. I stopped and passed the soap case to my left hand in order to make my salute. "You must run!" he barked, and gave me a smack. Blow number nine.

Today, we received a ration of milk for the second time, and it was wonderful after a bath. Octopus showed up at dinner tonight. It was delicious, but nevertheless I just want sweets. When it comes to food, we all snarl at each other like stray dogs. It's shameful, but we can't help it. And I find myself equally convinced by two contradictory theses. One holds that military life degrades you, and the other that it ennobles you. Two selves coexist inside me: a "noble" Yoshino, who would discipline his mind to the utmost of his ability, and an animalistic, base Yoshino. "It is evidence of a degraded character," I once read in a book by a Western philosopher, "to obsess oneself with food, drink, and other affairs of the body." At the time, I couldn't have agreed more. I even congratulated myself that, in the light of this philosophy, my own good character shone, but now I know how easily, and how quickly, such half-baked "nobility" crumbles. If anyone who has never undergone the ordeal we are suffering here ever crows these words of philosophy to me, I will certainly bite his nose. At a time like this, how can we *not* obsess over a precious bag of candy?

I experience pleasure when I take a bath, eat a snack, or change my undershirt. I take pleasure in the hum of a lark I noticed while advancing, on all fours, in a trying battle drill. It is a blessing that I find such bliss in insignificant things—things I always took for granted.

From the looks of it, the larks are immune to the common cold now running its course among us. Full of life, they sing their songs of spring, and are free. As for me, I take medication every morning, a Brocin solution and a stomach remedy called Adsorbin.

After the nightly study session, I joined the astronomy workshop. The clouds of the day had retreated, leaving behind them a beautiful starry sky. I learned to identify Cassiopeia, Orion, Andromeda, Perseus, and so on. It disquiets me a little to think that, a few months from now, we must fly over enemy territory, navigating by the light of these stars. All the same, gazing up into the sky seemed somehow to evoke a fine fellow-feeling among us. Even the instructors spoke with a strangely casual and intimate air. It was nice.

I watched as Douglases, Y20 "Ginga" bombers, navy Type-96 land-based attack bombers, and various trainers flew across the night sky, each at its characteristic speed, each with its characteristic roar. Their red and blue identification lights made streaks in the sky, and from where I stood I could plainly see the purple flash of the engines. The instructor who'd been at Rabaul expressed his deep regrets about those flashes, though. These telltale purple lights, he said, make it extremely hard for Japanese planes to conduct nighttime raids. U.S. aircraft don't have this problem.

After we were dismissed, Wakatsuki, a guy in my outfit from Takushoku University, was happily chanting a Chinese poem, eyes cast down toward the drill ground, when a deck officer accosted him. "Stop pining for the outside world!" the officer quipped, and struck him twice. Wakatsuki returned to the barracks wearing a stupefied look. He had thought he had been displaying his true Japanese spirit.

The weather is utterly changeable. The night before last was awfully hot and humid, and we all broke out in a greasy sweat as we slept. I rose in the middle of the night and removed my shirt and drawers. Then last night, abruptly, we had a snowstorm. Flakes blew in through gaps in the windows, piling up inside the barracks. We got twelve centimeters in total, but today the sun shone. Mt. Tsukuba was all white.

A number of packages arrived yesterday and today, but most of the contents were confiscated. Hardly anything made its way to us. I received a package too, and I found myself presented with a pair of woolen socks. But everything else was seized.

Akame, the assistant division officer, failed to turn up at dinner. It was Fujikura's turn to serve the meal, so he carried the officer's dinner to his room. There, Fujikura beheld on the desk a mountain of confiscated treats—navel oranges, jellied bean paste, rice crackers, chocolates, and cans of fruit cocktail. No wonder the man hadn't come to dinner. "It sure looked good," Fujikura reported.

Yesterday, Wakatsuki was made to open his parcel in front of the assistant officer. He cut the string and out spilled roasted peanuts, all over the floor. "Throw those away," the officer ordered. Wakatsuki swept the peanuts into a dustpan, but on his way to the incinerator he managed to wolf them all down, together with their fresh coating of dirt. No doubt that accounts for the severe diarrhea he has been experiencing all day. A copy of the *Weekly Asahi* was sent for N., but that, too, was confiscated. Only the wrapper made its way to the addressee. I don't see why they should seize a magazine like the *Asahi*. Someday

I will enter the teaching profession, and the way these instructors behave, including Akame, gives me food for thought.

In the afternoon they passed out cards on which we were to indicate whether we prefer to train for piloting or reconnaissance. Without hesitation I put myself down for piloting. Fujikura and Sakai did the same. I expected Fujikura to go for reconnaissance, judging from his words and deeds, because it carries a somewhat lower risk, but I was wrong. We are to take a Morse code test from 1730 to 1840 tomorrow, the results of which will figure into the decision as to who is assigned to the flight group and who to the recon group.

I also filed an application to buy a sword. With any luck I should be able to get a stainless steel *Kamakura* or *Kikusui* sword.

It seems like the date for our departure is finally drawing near, though the talk about our leaving the base at the end of March was nothing but a groundless rumor after all. I saw the calendar in the instructors' room. The schedule is chock full through the whole month of April.

MARCH 26

At 8:30, we fell in for an outing. Those who hadn't pressed their pants under the bedding, or whose socks were dirty, or who hadn't shaved or polished the heels of their shoes, were ordered to take a step forward. Each received a blow of correction from the division officer.

At quarter past nine, we were finally granted liberty. We passed through the gate and walked, one by one, for four kilometers along the Navy Road to the railroad station. They say that if you go up to the rooftop of the administration building on a liberty day, you can see a line of navy-blue military uniforms strung out from the base to the town like a procession of ants. Enlisted men gave me crisp salutes, and I acknowledged them with stiff ones of my own, feeling like an officer for the first time. We are commanded, most sternly, to preserve our honor as officers, yet we are hardly ever treated like officers at all. I don't want to take a cynical view of the matter, but if the navy manages to send us all so willingly into the jaws of death simply by giving us an officers' uniform—well, I must say they are doing it on the cheap.

At a used bookstore in town I came across a series of annotations of unpublished classic Japanese literature, but I passed it by, feeling no longer connected to things like that. The time left to me is short and priceless. I know that. I just don't know what to do about it, other than to grow ever more anxious.

We must not drink, we must not enter a restaurant, we must not talk to the ranks, and we must not stray from our designated area. Come to think about it, we are not allowed to do anything at all.

I walked over to Tsuchiura House, the designated officers' club, at a little after 10:30. More than ten men were packed into a tiny room of just four-and-a half tatami mats. This tatami room was so cramped that I could hardly stretch my legs, and once I finished the lunch and the fried-dough cookies I had brought with me, there was nothing else to do. The tea was first-rate, though.

In the afternoon I went to the railway station. I watched the southbound and northbound trains come and go, as the station attendant cried out, "Tsuchiura-a-a, Tsuchiura-a-a!" I bought a platform ticket and roamed around the waiting room, gazing

BURIAL IN THE CLOUDS

blankly at the crowd for quite some time. The burning smell the brakes give off as the trains grind to a halt, the odor of the toilets—all of it made me nostalgic. A hazy heat shimmered over the tracks, and, vacantly, I imagined that the rails ran all the way through to Kyoto and Osaka, without interruption.

I dropped into a photo studio before heading back and had a picture taken to send home, and also to Professor O. Plum flowers bloomed on the hillside, and the barley fields were a beautiful green, though the grain is not yet tall. Still, I was dreadfully hungry, my legs were exhausted, and for some reason I arrived back at the air station utterly disenchanted. I never expected my long-awaited first outing to be so joyless.

We mustered at 1600 after returning to base, and sang martial songs. I hear that, up until a few years ago, outings inevitably meant a windfall of food. Singing carried the added benefit of aiding the digestion, and therefore of preventing what used to be called "Monday catarrh." For us, that sort of thing is nothing but a dream.

After dinner I helped transplant a cherry tree to make room for an air-raid shelter. I saw two frogs hibernating in the earth.

APRIL 1

The summer schedule started today. Reveille at 0515.

Glider training is now in full swing, as are examinations designed to sort out the pilots from the reconnaissance men. Yesterday I had my first real airborne experience. I probably flew ten meters. I can't quite control my foot, and no matter how many times I try, the rudder bar always slants to the left. My plane turns left, banks off with its nose tipped down, and hits the runway.

Judging from this performance, it's doubtful whether I'll make it into the pilot's group.

Starting at 0745 we underwent what they call a "morphological character examination." This was done by a visiting physiognomist. First he smeared our hands with mimeograph ink to take fingerprints and palm-prints. Then he read our palms, scrutinized the shape of our heads, and studied every aspect of our faces, turning us sideways and backwards. Afterwards they seated each of us on a swivel chair (rather like a barber's) and whirled it around like all fury. Then, using a stopwatch, they timed us to see how long it took each one of us to walk a straight line and stand at attention. It seems I'm rather good at this. Those who have a defect in the inner ear, or some other physical impairment, collapsed the moment they staggered off the chair, groveling about for a spell like an animal.

The meteorology course began today.

We were given *manju* with white bean paste as a snack—a very rare occasion. It was delicious.

APRIL 4

Lectures on "ship identification" began today. Finally we are getting some practical knowledge of the war. There are battleships of the *West Virginia* type, aircraft carriers of the *Saratoga* and *Hornet* types, *Chicago*-class cruisers, and so forth.

Incidentally, I read over my own journal today, and it unsettled me. Recently (or so I convinced myself, anyway) I have adopted a rather intrepid attitude with respect to death. However, I find that on March 19 I wrote: "Someday I will enter the teaching profession. . . ." Evidently I "think" that I must die, but all the while "feel" that I will surely return home alive. True enough, it gets my hackles up when, at every opportunity, our instructors tell us we must die. But really, it is high time I looked death squarely in the face and steered my mind toward it.

A postcard arrived from Kashima, and I read it over and over again. "Let us end our brief lives together," he writes, "happily, gracefully, and meaningfully." I was moved to see that Kashima had at last arrived at such a sentiment. I am certain he wouldn't say these things merely to please the censors. I mustn't fall behind him.

The study session was canceled this evening so that a truly singular man could deliver a lecture. The other day we had a physiognomist, and tonight it was this fox-like orator, this Mr. Gakushu Ohara of the Association for Enhancement of Imperial National Prestige. He is a meager-looking man, about forty years old. He made so many references to ancient texts the— *Manyoshu*, the *Kojiki*, Shinto prayers—that his lecture amounted to little more than a succession of esoteric phrases like "*sumerami ikusa*," "*kan-nagara no michi*," "*kakemakumo ayani totoki*," and so on, and it was all perfect nonsense to me. Whenever he uttered the phrase *kamemakumo ayani totoki* (or, *we must speak it only in utmost reverence*), a reference to the imperial family inevitably followed, and this required us all to assume, each time, a 'ten-hut! posture in our seats. It was bothersome in the extreme. The man is indiscriminately fanatical, and often sounds as if he is chanting. And indeed, he *did* chant occasionally, joining his palms together. "*A-a-amaterasu o-o-mikami-i*, Goddess of the Sun. . . ." None of us students took him seriously. Some snickered, some took out paperbacks to read, and still others snored away. I dozed off myself, halfway through. Several men farted. This gibberish dragged on for two and a half hours, and just when I thought it was finally ending, Ohara announced, "Now I'd like you all to purify yourselves in the waters of Lake Kasumiga-ura." It was already past nine! Give me a break!! In any case, the division officer dashed over to confer with the executive officer, with the result that the proposal was declined, after all, on the pretext that "a bad cold was going around." Who on earth got the idea of inviting such a man to speak?

But no sooner had we seen the lecturer off than the order came. "All hands turn out on the drill ground immediately! On the double!" I knew something was coming, and sure enough, the division officer mounted the platform and spoke.

"However the lecture was"—obviously he didn't think he had heard a fine piece of talking either—"you should have known better. What's with this attitude of yours anyway? All those who drifted off and passed gas, step forward now!"

Instantly, a hush descended upon us, which two men broke with their footsteps.

"There have to be many, many more. Come forward!"

I had itchy feet, but didn't go after all.

"So, you men don't have the backbone to come forward!" the division officer said. "Once, when I was at the Naval Academy, a midshipman farted during a moral lecture. The instructor ordered the perpetrator to show himself, and no less than five men came forward. The guest lecturer was thoroughly impressed. Your spirit is exactly contrary to theirs. The sixth division officer will take up the slack tonight!"

With that, the front and rear ranks of each division were made to face one another, and each of us was ordered to strike the man opposite him. If an officer determined that anyone was cutting corners, or going easy on his partner, he would say, "Hit him like this!" and damn well show you how till you collapsed. I faced Wakatsuki, a fellow who packs quite a punch. Curiously, the good beating had made me trigger-happy, and, at the command "Rear rank, go!" I smashed Wakatsuki's face in. Both of us left with bloody cuts on our lips.

They made the rounds at 2215, an hour and a half behind schedule.

APRIL 8

Father has written. Our goat gave birth to a kid. I guess they'll have plenty of goat's milk to drink. Also, the peas in the kitchen garden are doing well, and they'll be ready to eat sometime next month. I can picture the butterflies fluttering around the pea-flowers in the yard. There's been no word at all from my brother Bunkichi.

In the morning, we had a lecture on aerial ordnance, with particular attention to guidance systems. The instructor was Lieutenant Washimura, who barely escaped death during the strategic "advance" in New Guinea. Japanese ordnance, he tells us, is marred by defective instruments that were rushed into production, and which lag far behind American equipment. His words sank deep into my heart. Just think about our radar and our bombsights, he says, and you see how long a road Japan still has to travel. As for the battleship *Kirishima*, which went down in the Third Battle of the Solomon Islands: Unquestionably this was due to the unerring accuracy of our enemy's radar-assisted firepower. Our men were flustered, the lieutenant explains, not knowing where the shells were coming from, and in the confusion they lost the rudder, and, with it, control of the ship. Thus the *Kirishima* sank, all too easily.

"True, the navy expects much of you," Lieutenant Washimura said. "But in my view it's regrettable that the press bureau at Imperial Headquarters sees fit to keep us all intoxicated with the results of the Battle of Hawaii and the Malay campaign, trumpeting our successes with such fanfare, as if to the very crack of doom." Generally speaking, the instructors who have been in battle, and had a tough go of it, are quite unassuming, and there is nothing fanatical or desperate about them. Lieutenant Washimura, though, seems particularly philosophical. Really bad are the instructors who stay behind in the training units. They get used to being instructors and wind up like bitter old maids.

Lieutenant Washimura also told us a story about so-called "Australian pig." They were marching through the jungle of New Guinea in retreat, with nothing to eat or drink, when they stumbled across an army unit. These soldiers possessed a rare store of mouthwatering meat. They had gotten hold of an "Australian pig," they said, and would be happy to share it with the navy men. At first, the sailors were grateful for the windfall, but then they noticed a number of dead Japanese soldiers, whose bodies lay scattered here and there, along the path of retreat. Flesh from their backs and thighs had been carved out. The lieutenant did not say whether or not he ate any of the meat. He may have. What must it feel like to discover that you've just eaten human flesh? If I am starving to death, will I think, "Now that I have eaten it once, it doesn't make any difference if I do it again"? Will I?

Air defense training this afternoon, and then again this evening. We had to conduct it inside the building, on account of the rain.

I feel gloomy, which probably has something to do with that story about "Australian pig." Ordinarily, I should have been celebrating the *Kanbutsue* today, the anniversary of the Buddha's birth, with hydrangea tea. For the *Kanbutsue*, we build a little "flower temple" (so called because its roof is bedecked with blossoms) and enshrine a figure of the Baby Buddha inside it. Then we fill a bowl at its base with hydrangea tea, to be sprinkled over the Buddha with a dipper. That sort of thing is so remote from us now. Come to think of it, though, the *Kanbutsue* might be celebrated on April 8 of the old lunar calendar. I'm not sure about these things anymore.

APRIL 11

Antiaircraft drills immediately followed reveille. We were on Defense Condition 1 throughout the morning.

Glider training proceeded, while we maintained the high alert. My left foot is still stiff and gets tense easily, making the plane tilt leftward. This is no good. I still hope somehow to make the grade as a pilot. The word is that our scores in Morse code weigh heavily, and I do better at that by the day. So if I can remember to do my gliding with due care, I'll probably be okay. As for Morse code, I can now understand without difficulty the flashing signals that the Red Dragonflies out of Kasumiga-ura Naval Air Station exchange with ground control during their night flights.

The cherry buds are swelling. They appear much later hereabouts than they do in Tokyo and points further west, but nevertheless it is spring. We may not live to see another one, but I'd be content if only my chapped skin would heal, as it has been killing me each time I do the laundry. I saw the first swallow along the lake today.

Mail call was at lunchtime. I received four postcards in total, from Professor E. at Kyoto University, from father, from K. in Shizuoka, and from Kashima in Takeyama. Every card spoke of cherry blossoms, inadvertently bringing me tidings of flowers from scattered parts of the country. According to Professor E., the whole university is now poised for the decisive battle. The Law and Economics Faculties have gone to Shimane Prefecture, and the Science Faculties to Shiga, to do their labor service. The Faculty of Letters alone remains in Kyoto, having completed its service in March. In the morning, the students attend lectures in the core curriculum. Afternoons are devoted to military drills, after which students audit lectures on topics of their own choosing. Three acres of fallow ground on campus have been dug up, and the tennis courts will be reclaimed as potato fields. Cherry blossoms are in full bloom where K.'s Chubu 3rd column is stationed in Shizuoka. Kashima sent me a heartfelt letter, not exactly in his usual tone.

"The Miura Peninsula is a stretch of hilly terrain," he wrote, "with a few copses scattered here and there. The cherry blossoms are out. To my right lies the ever-blue Sea of Sagami, over which I can see Mt. Fuji on a sunny day. There are no cherry trees on the barracks grounds, but *kirishima* azaleas, torch azaleas, tulips, pansies, daisies, and other such things grow riotously in the newly built beds. Looking at these flowers blooming in the sun comforts my weary heart. I'm always thinking about you guys. I suppose I now regret a little that I was judged 'not flight-worthy' and ended up here alone, separated from you all."

I showed the postcards from Professor E. and Kashima to Fujikura. He looked dismayed and said he hadn't received any. Well, what can I say? He doesn't write to anyone. He did say, however, that he plans to write a long letter to Professor E., once his assignment as a pilot comes through. He intends to send it through some back channel in order to avoid the censors, who would by no means approve it.

After dinner I went to see the newsreel, ditty box in hand. It's just like the military to make us all run twenty minutes' distance simply to watch a ten-minute film. But what I saw in the newsreel was very interesting: commencement ceremonies at the Naval and Army Academies, young tank-men undergoing train-ing, a report on the progress of the war along the India/Burma border. Jogging back to my quarters, I met Fujikura again.

"Did you notice those Indian soldiers learning how to handle the high-angle gun?" he asked.

"Yeah, I did. I couldn't tell what they are thinking."

"I know. They were perfectly deadpan. And if I draw anything good from this war, that'll probably be it."

"What do you mean by that?" I asked.

"I can't whisper while running," he said. "I'll explain it to you later."

And that was all.

Maybe Fujikura isn't as devoted to his "ingenuity" as one might suppose, with all his cynical talk. In truth, he probably does his fair share of brooding and agonizing. Anyway, I don't have many occasions to chat privately even with the men in my own outfit, let alone with Fujikura, who is only in the same division.

The division officer admonished us during the study session, late this evening. "Military men, aircrews in particular, must rely on others to see to their personal effects when they are killed," he said. "You must exercise due care with your belongings. Be scrupulous. Take diaries, for instance. You are certainly free to keep one. But private though it may be, you have no control over who might read it someday. It's best, so far as you can manage it, never to write anything that might tarnish your name after death." This discountenanced me somewhat, as I keep a diary rather diligently. Would I be made a laughingstock if classmates, my instructors, or my subordinates were to read it after I die? Needless to say, the navy is hardly the beautiful, perfect world that schoolgirls dream about, and it is only fitting that I should record my honest criticism of it. On the other hand, I worry that this diary might clearly expose the weak, unsteady mind that I possess, in light of the hardships I am to face. I will have to train myself as much as I can, so that I can write exactly what I feel and think, and yet not open myself to shame. Even as I write this, though, the merest introspection gives rise to doubt, just as in that book *Santaro's Diary:* "You liar," comes the reproach, and pricks the hand that holds the pen. It is no small feat to leave behind a diary that is both "respectable" *and* sincere. But I will, after all, write from the heart, and make my petty complaints until all weakness fades away. And I shall be content if anyone reading my diary sees a student who has studied the *Manyoshu* at university agonize over his infirmities, but in the end meet his death without ambivalence, in the belief that *somehow*, anyway, he takes his part at the very foundation of his fatherland. If this diary stains my name in death, that can't be helped.

Or, if I learn that I am to make a sortie tomorrow, with little hope of coming back, I can always burn this notebook.

APRIL 23

I am infested with lice, and not just any ordinary lice, either. It's astonishing. I've heard a theory that this type of louse is sexually transmitted, but I haven't laid a finger on anybody. Clearly, I got them when I took a bath. I slipped into the toilet to inspect the situation in private, and there they were, buried under my hair, pale-colored pests with wriggling legs, so small I could hardly make them out. A number of these quite undesirable creatures clung to my flesh, biting into it. I scraped some off with my fingernails, and pressed them. They popped and bled. It's perfectly miserable. I am not suffering alone, though. Not a few students hereabouts are constantly scratching their groins, striking all manner of undignified poses.

"What are you scratching at!?" the division officer shouted at N. during battle drills this morning.

N. blushed deeply, but nevertheless seemed offended. "I got a dose of crabs at the petty officers' bath, sir," he began, but he couldn't finish his explanation before another shout came.

"Stop your whining!" the officer said. His tone notwithstanding, he seemed to be suppressing a chuckle. "Why don't you consult a doctor? Get some mercurial ointment at once."

"Yes, sir," N. replied, with a salute. He was all set to run, fists properly at his waist, when the thunder came:

"Idiot! Who the hell told you to get medical treatment for crab lice in the middle of a battle!?" And he dealt N. a blow. In nervous desperation, N. blushed even more deeply. My heart went out to him.

By contrast to the division officer, the drill instructors have the common touch after all. "Cadet Yoshino, you have crab lice, too, don't you?" they would say, grinning. My face was as red as N.'s.

During the break, Petty Officer First Class Okamoto, who is attached to the student units, triumphantly imparted to us his great stock of knowledge about this particular type of louse.

Crab lice, he says, are so named for their physical similarity to crabs. They are by nature lethargic, and if left undisturbed will simply stay put for days, biting into the skin under the hair. When immersed in hot water, though, some of the little buggers get startled and cut loose. They cruise around the surface, and, as this happens to be at about the same level as our private parts, they sink their teeth into yet another victim. We student reserves, Okamoto said, turn all red and white, making a mountain out of a molehill, when we suffer even a mild infestation, but it can be much worse if you are assigned to a fleet where water is in short supply. A destroyer, which has a canvas bath, is particularly bad. Let one person get infested and the lice spread to the entire crew. Nobody is bashful or self-conscious about it. They say the condition can be fatal if it spreads to the eyebrows or the head, but, he assured us, this is quite rare. Experienced petty officers find it gratifying to dig out the lice with a toothpick while baring their pubic regions to the setting sun after a bath. In this manner they rid themselves of six or seven lice at a time. A petty officer would never willingly resort to so indelicate a tactic as to eradicate the lice with mercurial ointment. All the same, if you really do want to root them out, mercurial ointment is the thing, and you should never, ever, shave your private parts. Etc. etc.

The special course this afternoon was sumo wrestling. The cherry trees on the base are finally in full bloom, and the rape blossoms are also out. Still, I can don a wrestler's loincloth, and the cherry blossoms can bloom, with rape blossoms in the bargain; but if it itches, it itches. My manners are not so delicate as those of Petty Officer First Class Okamoto. I will definitely visit the doctor's office tomorrow and get some mercurial ointment.

April 29, The Imperial Birthday

Rained in the early morning. But the sky cleared away beautifully around seven-thirty. No excursion today. We bowed in the direction of the Imperial Palace, and then did obeisance to His Majesty's photograph.

Sakai said: "Worshipping His Majesty's photograph with such dignity, and in military uniform—it all makes me feel so solemn and so firm. I'm certainly changing, and I take that as a blessing." To some extent, I share his feeling.

Sumo wrestling in the morning. The green turf looks exceptionally fresh after the rain, and the tender grass is strewn with the petals of the cherry blossoms. I treaded lightly over them, feeling almost as if I were committing a sacrilege. The clover, which had drawn up the water from the earth, felt soft and comfortable to my feet.

I saw a thunderhead cloud this afternoon. All of a sudden, the weather is like summer. Unit drilling from 1600. Tonight's study session was open. I used this week's postcard to write to Kashima.

Decisions as to who shall be pilots and who shall go into reconnaissance were announced today, as were also our new duty stations. I managed to make the grade as a pilot and am delighted from the bottom of my heart. The mercurial ointment completely eradicated that infamous infestation, so I feel refreshed in both mind and body. We were evenly divided into pilot and reconnaissance groups, and Sakai and Fujikura both belong to the first. I must bear in mind what an honor it is to be designated a pilot. Only some nine hundred out of three hundred thousand men conscripted into the Naval Air Corps in the emergency national call-up are judged fit to be pilots. Like it or not, we have now been geared, like toothed wheels, into the most crucial component of a huge machine, a machine that will affect the fate of our country and determine the outcome of the war. Crews of conventional planes are to be assigned to the naval air stations at Yatabe, Miho, and Izumi. As for myself, I am bound for Izumi, where the majority of the future pilots, six hundred of them, will also go. Izumi, I hear, is a small town along the Kagoshima main rail line, halfway between Kumamoto and Kagoshima.

Surely we will succeed in the important work entrusted to us. We need not necessarily take a grim view of the progress of the war. The 13th Class of student reserve fliers will bear up to hold the tide at its present level, and we of the 14th Class will make a rally. Today is the day of the Boy's Festival, and though we have neither rice dumplings nor carp streamers to mark the event, I feel a kind of manly pride. As for our day-to-day life at the new station: I should imagine we will be allowed more letters, and the food might be better, too. Before long we will be commissioned, and the gloom will be swept out of me. I know I had better not let my hopes run after my desires, lest I be disappointed, but what a delight it will be to leave this place! The word is we will be allowed visitors on the 14th. This might be the last chance we ever have to see our parents, so the division officer says we must be in good spirits, make the most of the occasion, and eat as much as we please—*ohagi*, red rice, what have you.

Strangely enough, today I had the queerest dream, at dawn, on the day of the announcement of our new assignments. I have never been superstitious, but from this point forward I can't help but believe in the separation of the soul from the body. I was back home in Osaka. I opened the door to the bookcase in my room, took from the right end of the second shelf my copy of *Poems for the Reverend Emperor,* and read it. I saw no one from my family. The blue curtain that hangs over the glass doors of the bookcase, however—*that* remains vividly before my eyes. I would be willing to say this was nothing but an ordinary dream if it weren't for that particular book, a book I had bought just before joining the navy, and which I had never had the chance to so much as open. But in my dream I opened it, and there can be no doubt that I read "San-ten-ka," a poem by an obscure author that deals with General Maresuke Nogi, a hero of the Russo-Japanese War, and his sons Katsusuke and Yasusuke. The poem celebrates the valor of both the father and the sons, and at one point in it the General, having escorted the great Emperor Meiji to the grave, puts into words his feelings toward his two sons, who had earlier fallen in battle. The following passage is particularly exquisite.

I am eternally grateful
To the late Emperor for his favors.
How can I bear to go home again now?
And the new Court has no need of councilors.
So, my old legs run after the funeral hearse.

Where are you, my sons?
Already I am eight years behind you in death.
But I am coming, together with your mother,
As we attend the Imperial hearse.
I am sorry to have made you wait so long.

I remembered the poem clearly from the dream. I found this so odd that I asked Wakatsuki, who happens to own the same book, to show me his copy, and as I turned to the page an uncanny sensation overcame me. The poem was just as I had seen it in my dream, almost to the letter. I do not know how to interpret this incident, other than to say that my soul left my body as I slept and returned to my hometown. If our souls do what our bodies plainly cannot, if they are endowed with perception as mine was in this dream, then I simply cannot believe that the complex activity of the mind is extinguished at the point of death, or that it is buried in the grave with the flesh. This notion heartens me, and gives me courage. Most definitely some sort of kinship affiliates sleep and death, and the question might not necessarily lie beyond the reach of science. Instead, this may be a matter that awaits scientific confirmation at a future date. Simply because science cannot at present explain a thing, and for that reason takes a dismissive view of it, we shouldn't sweep it all aside as "superstition." At least, I certainly cannot disregard the miraculous dream I had this morning.

Notes by Akira Fujikura
May, Showa 19 (1944) Tsuchiura Naval Air Station

Professor E.

Please excuse me for ever having been so discourteous. It has been quite a long time since I sent you so much as a simple greeting. In fact, it was right after I first joined the navy, at Otake, and all the while I have been receiving kind letters from you.

I assume that you have already heard from Yoshino or Sakai that we are allowed only one postcard per week. That is one of my excuses, but there was another reason why I chose not to write you for such a long time. So far as my parents and siblings are concerned, I can content myself with saying to them the sorts of things the censors permit us all to say, but I simply could not persuade myself to send so artificial a note to you. For the same reason, I have scarcely written to my oldest and closest friends. Of course, there were times when I almost wrote you to say that I was dashing about, right as rain, hopping into gliders, shouldering heavy machine guns, and gripping the fat oars of a cutter, that my weight had risen to sixty-five kilograms, and that I enjoyed splendid health, and often recalled debating with you as we ate pork cutlet at Ogawa-tei. But each time the result was peculiarly hollow, and each time I tore up the letter and trashed it. Sure, I remember the pork cutlet at Ogawa-tei, and I now weigh sixty-five kilograms. It's all true enough. But I couldn't banish the thought that there is something else I must write, something of my true feelings—something of which I want you, at least, to have some knowledge before I end this life of mine (which might not last much longer).

There is no reason I should be so ceremonious, but that, anyway, is why I have chosen to write for you, bit by bit, and as I find time to spare, something between a letter and a note of my impressions, and to send it all to you once it is done. And I shall be grateful if you accept my complaints as those of a man who harbors his warped, unspoken views and can direct them to no one else. Needless to say, this letter would never pass the censors. However, we will leave Tsuchiura Air Station soon for a flight training base in a town called Izumi, way down in Kagoshima. We should be allowed to see our families, if only briefly, during the journey, at Shinagawa Station in Tokyo, and, in Kansai, either at Kyoto, Osaka, or Kobe Stations. My thought is that on one of these occasions I may have a chance to deliver this letter to you by means of someone I can trust. With that hope in mind, I've started writing today.

It has been exactly five months to the day since we joined the navy. My life here is utterly lonely. To be lonely in the military is most peculiar, it seems. I live in close contact with the naked flesh of hundreds, even thousands, of other men, shoulder to shoulder, day and night, leading a lively, tumultuous life, always on the move. But when I escape for a moment from all the rush, an overpowering desolation cuts me deep, as if I were totally abandoned in an empty, tranquil wilderness. My heart bonds with nothing, never once have I laid bare my feelings. This loneliness differs completely in nature from the solitude I knew as I studied in my second floor, four-and-a-half tatami room in the Hyakumanben district near Kyoto University, warming my hands over a hibachi on cold winter nights, yet satisfied in the belief that I was doing work that related to the world.

BURIAL IN THE CLOUDS

My only consolation is that Sakai and Yoshino are here with me. Still, I rarely get the chance to speak with them in a relaxed sort of way. Besides, both men have changed considerably, each in his own way, over the course of the last five months. As a matter of fact, this place changes every living soul. We have ceased to talk about the *Manyoshu.* Everyone is trying his best, under a bitter trial, to find some sort of anchorage. I am by no means being sarcastic when I say that Sakai and Yoshino are, after all, uncommonly modest and supple at heart, compared to myself. We know that in order to survive as military men or as naval officers, and above all to face the shadow of death that looms before our eyes, we must have a firm sense of ourselves. We accept that, obediently. In fact, we are more than willing to re-create ourselves for the purpose at hand, when all we ever get drilled into us, by the chief instructor, the division officers, the flight instructors, the daily newspapers with their infamous tone and their conveniently selected extracts from books, is the necessity of carrying through this holy war to its end, our responsibilities as honorable youths, the glorious tradition of the Imperial Navy, and the ideal of "the whole world under one roof." Neither Sakai nor Yoshino has ever been blindly fanatical, and I wouldn't necessarily call them that now, but their critical, skeptical air seems to be diminishing with repeated exposure to all these mantras. First, they began to think that the slogans weren't *entirely* empty, then they were persuaded that they actually made some sense, and finally they came to believe that these slogans were absolutely right, and that all along only their own "deficient consciousness" prevented them from seeing the light. At least, they seem to be moving in this direction. I stand alone in my pigheaded inability to abandon my suspicions. I could never assume the "spiritual" frame of mind that the instructors demand of me, and yet I can't figure out for sure what to do about my future. In point of fact, that timid Sakai (and maybe this is precisely *because* he is timid) recently declared that he has begun to fathom the deep meaning of the phrase, "We shall be united into a single Emperor." He is even prepared to espouse the theory that we never truly understood the *Manyoshu,* which is, after all, a collection of "ethnic" poems, because we failed to comprehend this great spirit of "being united into a single Emperor."

Several days ago, Yoshino came to me with a somber look on his face and reported a dream he had had. He tells me that his soul left his body while he slept, and traveled to his home in Osaka. He says that, while there, it read *Poems for the Reverend Emperor,* which Yoshino himself had never read before, and that, now, he vividly remembers the lines of a poem in it. Yoshino was shaken. Maybe he has already sent you a postcard describing this incident. What touched me, though, was how thoroughly Yoshino struggles, thinking, as he takes matters so hard, that he must stir in himself a spirit of martyrdom, and that he must train himself up. No doubt he is anything but insincere. I can tell that by his look. Yet I think it highly symbolic that what Yoshino supposedly did, among all the other things he could have done, and would have wanted to do, at his old house, was read a bit of the *Poems for the Reverend Emperor,* such-and-such a poem celebrating the martyrdom of General Nogi. It was fortunate that Yoshino's soul wasn't caught when it went AWOL and given a blow by the rigorous guard commander at Tsuchiura Naval Air Station. Interestingly enough, though, in Yoshino's outfit there is a geeky fellow named Wakatsuki from Takushoku University, and he has had in his possession, for some time now, this same book, volume one of *Poems for the Reverend Emperor*. Anyway, to me, it seems far more rational to suppose that Yoshino had read this poem a long time back, and had simply forgotten about it until it put in an appearance in his dream, than that his soul made an excursion to Osaka.

About a month ago, a Mr. Gakushu Ohara from the Association for the Enhancement of Imperial National Prestige visited our base, and gave a fanatical talk, pure gibberish, for two and a half hours, earning the ridicule of everyone present. He was one of those inspired leaders of whom there is an epidemic these days, the same genre of men you often complained about. Yoshino and Sakai were both scornful. But when things reach this point, we can't content ourselves with sneering at Mr. Ohara alone, I think. Besides, fellows like this Mr. Something Ohara reap tidy profits making the rounds of the military training units and the schools, giving their "inspirational" speeches, and performing their "purifications." And who knows, they may be perfect realists at heart, all the while laughing into their sleeves. But Sakai and Yoshino aren't of a calculating turn of mind, and that makes me more apprehensive about them.

Professor E.

I know I wasn't a very good student. I often put on airs, and now and then I launched into arguments against the theories of all you scholars out of conceit. Consequently, I was never a favorite with the professors. Many a time I wished I could, and thought I *must*, have an open, cheerful, supple mind, just like all the other students, but now I'm determined to stick to this cranky, arrogant disposition of mine. Only extraordinary crankiness can save you from being cajoled into the belief (and this, mind you, while leading the kind of life we lead here) that the war is indeed a great mission given to us by our country, and that our country will be saved by our martyrdom. Things will change someday. Our desperate feelings may not be understood forever, either by the older generation or the younger. Still, whenever I get the chance to see Yoshino and Sakai in private, I tell them, in the strongest terms possible, just how foolish it is to force themselves, and so rapidly, too, to change their way of thinking. Occasionally, after giving the matter some thought, they say, "You are right," and we all agree in criticizing certain aspects of navy life and the general conduct of the war. But for the most part, they (Yoshino in particular) will not budge an inch, saying, "Still, at this point anyway, Japan must win the war. I take it to heart, as a Japanese citizen, that we must fight it all out, with the fate of our race at stake. It's a supreme duty. You can't quarrel with it. Our country will collapse if each of us starts to express his own particular view and turns his back." Gazing into Yoshino's earnest face makes me falter somewhat. It is true, the war is "in progress," however wrong it may be. And though, as I say, I oppose the war and don't want any longer to be a cog in its machinery, I can make no concrete answer if asked what it is I believe I should do. One possible course of action is simply to try to save my own life. Shrewd as I am, however, it would be extremely difficult for me, a navy pilot, alone to escape death. It's not that I'll be killed unless I finish off the enemy first. No, I'll be eliminated whether or not I kill the enemy. It's not that

BURIAL IN THE CLOUDS

my friends will die unless I do. No, *everybody* must die, my friends, me, one and all. That such total war is our destiny I take for granted. Needless to say, I'm not prepared in the least.

I know I should explain to you why I ever volunteered to be a pilot, given the beliefs I hold. But I don't have the courage to commit my thoughts about that to paper, not, anyway, until I have come to terms with my feelings in some measure. Be that as it may, at least I can say that part of the reason was my more or less irresponsible and apathetic attitude. Whichever course I took, I thought, piloting or reconnaissance, I wouldn't have any control at all over my own life and death. To put it plainly, there was simply no guarantee whatsoever of my safe return, even if I went into reconnaissance.

Professor E.

I fear that you may be deeply disturbed on receiving this sloppily penciled letter. First of all, it must annoy you to read my illegible scrawl, and second, you may well feel that it is dangerous to have such a letter on hand. Please burn it when you are through. I don't really believe, though, that what I say is especially dangerous or immoral, while I *do* concede that my writing is culpably verbose. Anyway, if we must endure such inconveniences, and run such risks, simply to think, say, and record thoughts as innocent as these, I have to wonder: What good can come of the civilization that my generation produces?

Well, now that I have begun, I will go ahead and say it. Lately I am all but convinced that we will lose this war. Don't you agree? We are just a bunch of student reserves, still in training, but simply because we are now under the flag, and are quasi-officers, we regularly hear what appears to be confidential intelligence, of which you teachers are likely unaware. And judging from these scraps of information, it seems perfectly clear that, so far as materiel is concerned, the gap between Japan and America beggars belief. Japan lost most of the main force of her aircraft carriers in the Battle of Midway Island. Ninety-nine percent of our ace pilots, who had displayed skills unparalleled in the world at the beginning of the war, were killed in the air battle over the Solomon Sea. Due to changes in the complexion of naval combat, we have already passed the stage at which the super-dreadnoughts *Yamato* and *Musashi* might have demonstrated their capabilities. On the other hand, I hear that America, flush with her technological superiority in ordnance and radar, is steadily completing new armaments of terrifying scale. What is more, our line of defense in the southeastern theater is rapidly losing ground. I find it ironic that the tide of war has turned in this way, given that the U.S. Navy is said to do its utmost to save its crews' lives, while the Japanese Imperial Navy still instructs its men that their entire duty is to die. Unless this war develops into some kind of "romantic" battle, in which a loyal subject emerges out of nowhere to lead our country to victory under his banner, it seems to me that Japan has no choice left but to carry its deteriorating military position forward to defeat. And I don't think the end will be long in coming. This is no "Ten Years' War" or "Hundred Years' War," as they sometimes say. I suspect that the war will be over within three years or so. And what if we manage to live that long, I sometimes fancy? Then Sakai, Yoshino, and the three hundred thousand odd students conscripted in the emergency call-up shall all be awakened from this hypnosis of war. And we shall find ourselves living in a defeated nation, Japan. The idea is so painful, even to me, that I can't bear to imagine what the country will be like. But somehow we will make our way back to you, and to our old university in Kyoto. Well, I guess that's just a fantasy after all. It will not happen. It's too much, even for me, to assume that we will be alive three years down the road.

Professor E.

Ten days have passed since I started to write this clumsy letter during study sessions, avoiding the eyes of my instructors. We have been to the village of Obata at the foot of Mt. Tsukuba, about thirty kilometers distant, for three days of maneuvers, from the day before yesterday until today. We rose at 4:30 on the morning of the departure, shouldered our rain gear, clipped haversacks and canteens to our waists, took up our #38 rifles, and assembled in front of the drill platform in the darkness of dawn. ("#38" means *old*, by the way. This rifle hasn't been updated since the 38th year of the Meiji era, in 1905.) The chief instructor almost shouted when he addressed us. "You are outfitted exactly as were your comrades who died their warriors' deaths at Makin, at Tarawa, and in the Aleutian Islands. Brace yourselves. Tough it out with fire and spirit during these next three days of maneuvers." By all appearances many among us *did* gird themselves up at this speech, burning with a *Damn the torpedoes, full speed ahead!* sort of intensity. And in point of fact, we all "toughed it out," without a single man dropping. But even an affair like this seems funny to me. Why should we find it moving rather than depressing, and how can it give us good reason to get all fired up, simply to be outfitted exactly like our hapless "comrades" who were ill-equipped, and, consequently, annihilated by our enemy's overwhelming firepower? I just can't help feeling that everything is standing wrong side up somehow.

Have you visited the country around here, by the way? Paulownia and wisteria were flowering gracefully in the prosperous villages at the foot of Mt. Tsukuba. Milk vetches were also in bloom, and frogs croaked in the rice fields. This is the spot where the poems in volume fourteen of the *Manyoshu* are set. As I lay in ambush under a chestnut tree, I tore off a Japanese pepper leaf and sniffed it, thinking, for no special reason, of the poem that says,

> Unlike the waters that thunder
> Against the rocks of Mt. Tsukuba,
> My heart never wavers.

On our way back, we practiced an intense running engagement. The rifle butt bit into my shoulder, my fatigues were thoroughly mired, and my face broke out in a salty sweat. Now I realize how aptly put the expression "My legs are like lead" really is. So I have no words to describe the euphoria I felt when, after returning to base, after finishing the laundry and cleaning duty, and after taking a bath, I received a parcel of sweets. But then I heard a fellow in my outfit say, while nibbling away at some confection, "It was tough, but it was good experience." I wanted to turn on him and had to struggle to suppress the urge. Isn't it the luxury of those who look forward to a long life to say that hard times make for "good experience"? As for me, the hard times I have here are just hard times plain and simple, and I cannot by any means imagine they will bear good fruit in the future.

Professor E.

I'm writing the last part of this letter on the train. Today is May 25. We are supposed to pass through Kyoto around five o'clock tomorrow morning. You will be sleeping peacefully in your Kita Shirakawa residence. At the moment, we are running halfway between Odawara and Atami, with the ocean on our left. I can see Kashima's Miura Peninsula looming low. A little while ago, I spotted a bunch of sorrel, a familiar face from the *Manyo* lectures, flowering along the railroad. The day after tomorrow we finally start our lives as real pilots in Izumi, down in southern Kyushu.

My heart is full, so I hope you will excuse me for writing out my scattered, incoherent thoughts at such length. As for the place where we may receive visitors, after many changes, they decided on Himeji Station, and the time appointed for it is tomorrow morning. My father should be there to see me. He is the kind of man who deeply reveres the Emperor and the Imperial Army and Navy, while he also respects you and Professor O. It makes me a little anxious, but I think I will ask him to deliver this letter to you. If the instructors watch us so closely that I can't carry out my plan, I will burn it in the toilet on the train. If this letter does happen to reach you, please destroy it after reading it through, as I said earlier.

Together with a few other students in his outfit, Yoshino is playing an old child's game with a handkerchief. Sakai is in another car. I can't see him from where I sit.

Professor, now I must bid you goodbye until I can write again. With best wishes for your good health and happiness.

JUNE 3 (CONTINUED FROM YOSHINO'S DIARY)

Flying is becoming the be-all and end-all of our lives.

Each of us has already received an air log and a flight record. Outfitted with an oil-stained flying suit, aviation cap, half boots, a pair of goggles, and a life jacket, every last one of us is, to all appearances, an imposing "warbird" of the Imperial Navy.

The schedule is exacting. Reveille is at 0530, and we assemble within two minutes after that. Seconds count if you must fold your blanket neatly on your bunk, tie your shoelaces tightly, and line up, all in two minutes flat. We are constantly on the run. Once I saw a newsreel about young trainee pilots. Watching them dash like madmen from one task to another, I thought the scene simply had to have been staged. Nothing could be further from the truth.

We are told that pilots must always keep a clear head. Should so much as a wisp of a cloud pass through a pilot's mind, he will inevitably lose control of his plane. They say pilots with fiancées back home have more accidents.

We live on a kind of tangent with death. We have to shout at the top of our lungs whenever we give account of ourselves, and if we let our guard down just a bit, we draw a storm of slaps before we cause an accident. The 13th Class of student reserves, now already commissioned, has stayed on as assistant division officers for the sea-plane units. They are a rough, bloodthirsty lot, and stick it to us the second they find us derelict. "Hold it right there, student of the 14th Class!" they will say, and over they come at a clip with a beating to complement the scolding. "Do you want to disgrace the Student Reserve Corps?!"

We were separated into boarding groups. I was assigned to group ten and took my first orientation flight today with Instructor Yamaguchi. The command to "Commence!" came at 1045, and off I sprinted to the aircraft. I thought I acted with composure and celerity, but obviously I lost my calm, since it wasn't until we were up in the air that I realized I wasn't wearing gloves. We flew at an altitude of 200 meters. That's about eight times the height of the Marubutsu Department Store in front of Shichijo Station, but it didn't feel particularly high, it just felt as if my body were suspended in air. There was something gratifying about the experience, making me wish very much to congratulate myself. Ahead of us was Instructor Ejiri's plane, floating along with Sakai aboard. I was pretty much disoriented as to our bearings, but as I steadied myself and took a close look, I noticed our position gradually shifting against the green background of the mountains. Beneath us ran streams. A grid lay over the land, with its roadways and airplane hangars, and that clear geometric pattern was dotted with men who looked like black beans. The barley in that lower world is ripe for harvest. We soon reached the turning point and changed direction, flying out over the sea, where I saw the islands of Amakusa, and their shorelines. The islands are exquisite, hemmed in by thin white ribbons of surf. The wide expanse of blue water swelled out, and the horizon seemed to recede as we moved on.

It was clear and sunny all day today. I felt not the slightest anxiety from takeoff to landing. It was exhilarating. We cut into the wind as we descended, and all of a sudden, each solitary blade of grass came into clear view, as when a camera snaps into focus. Next I saw the grass pressed down by the wind, and in a split second my feet were on the ground. Who would believe that just five or ten meters of lovely green grass during a landing, or a variation of just three to five degrees in inclination, can mark the difference between life and death?

I felt fairly well accustomed to flying my second and third times up, but during the third flight the wind shifted abruptly from east to west, somewhere around the fourth turning point, just before we started our descent. Without warning I lurched 180 degrees into a vertical turn. Before I knew it, the sky and the earth were at my sides and the horizon slipped at a right angle before my eyes. I didn't know up from down or right from left. A thrill of horror shot through me, but of course we landed safely all the same. I flew three times, for a total of twenty-two minutes in the air. This duration is recorded in a log, and once our accumulated flight time reaches three or four hundred hours, we should be full-fledged pilots, capable of manipulating the plane as if it were an extension of the body.

Attaining for the first time a bird's-eye view of the sea, and of the mountains of southern Kyushu, I know what Nagata-no-Okimi felt when he sang (in volume three of the *Manyoshu*),

> The narrows of Satsuma,
> The home of the Hayahito folk
> Far beyond the clouds:
> All of this I saw today.

Izumi is some two and a half hours by express train from Kagoshima, via Ijuin, Sendai, and Akune, and it is a place of utter scenic beauty. Izumi looks across the Shiranui Sea to Amakusa, and the Koshiki-jima Islands lie off to the southwest. Beyond the sprawling airstrip of green grass you can see the silvery waves, even when you are standing on the ground. A lark has built a nest in the grass, and it sings as it flies, soaring as high as the planes.

Discipline is severe, the flying suits are stifling, and it's no easy trick to sprint with the contents of your leg pockets kicking around. But we are all in high spirits. I clean forgot my birthday on May 30. I didn't notice the day had passed until I was ordered to fill out a statement giving my personal history and background last night, and I'm actually pleased about this. I am twenty-four years old now.

The *Hagakure*, a book on *bushido*, says, "To conquer your enemy, first conquer your friends. To conquer your friends, first conquer yourself. To conquer yourself, first conquer your body with your mind." Whenever I caught even the slightest cold, I used to burrow under the covers, giving myself up to sloth, and I haven't entirely vanquished the more indolent aspects of my character. But I really must rid myself of them soon, if I am ever to die a worthwhile death for my country, or if I am to discipline myself into maturity as a pilot in time.

JUNE 11

Excursion from 0800. Generally, Kyushu is very well supplied, and our outings will be far more enjoyable than those we made in Tsuchiura. I wish mother could try one of the steamed yam-paste buns they make at the Brotherhood of Enlisted Men.

I had five bowls of sweet *shiruko,* drank four glasses of Calpis, and ate a parcel of snacks, a bowl of *udon,* and ten *manju* with yam-paste. Then I met Fujikura and Sakai, as we had earlier arranged, and walked with them from the Brotherhood out to Komenotsu, breaking a sweat under the early summer sun. Along the way we saw fields of ripe barley, the sprightly children of Kyushu, all tanned and barefoot, and then the bright sea beyond.

They say Komenotsu used to prosper as the point of export for rice produced all over these plains, but now it is a little fishing port renowned for its fine tiger prawns. We decided to leave the prawns for a later date and catch a train to Minamata. I heard that to the east of Komenotsu lies the site of the barrier of Noma, which runs along the northern border of the old Satsuma Clan, but we decided to save that for another day, too. Incidentally, as we walked from Izumi to Komenotsu, Fujikura started in with his constant complaint, claiming that Sakai and I had changed, and disagreeably, too.

"You say Japan will rally once we toe the line," Fujikura said. "You say you will die honorably. Is this really, honestly, what you both think?" Who wouldn't feel antagonized when challenged like this? So we fell to arguing. Essentially, all Fujikura wants to convey is his general opposition to the war, or at any rate his extremely pessimistic outlook as to its progress. He maintains that there is no good reason why we, having been drawn into this conflict through no choice of our own, should believe we must die for our country. His attitude also seems rather irresponsible and apathetic, and he basically says that nothing good will happen to Japan anyway, whether we die honorably or not.

"You despise fanaticism. You hate the foolish opportunism of all the scholars," Fujikura continued. "But you fail to recognize that you are losing your own minds." He does go on and is devious in the way he expresses his estimable opinions, though, and he didn't used to be like this. Fujikura, too, may be losing his mind.

"But we *can* carry the war through," I argued, "precisely *because* we are all just a little bit mad. That's what the circumstances require." Fujikura shot me a contemptuous look, but what does he believe we ought to do? This conversation makes me want to know, for once and for all, just how he thinks we should live—just how he thinks we should conduct ourselves, given our present situation.

"If you can figure out a way to save your own life," he says, "then you can make it through. Don't lose your head. Hold to your beliefs, and if there really is no way out of this mess, at least never give up your consciousness and your pride. When I say 'consciousness,' I have something rather different in mind from what you mean by the word." I understand that Fujikura can really let loose only when he is alone with the three of us. We mustn't cut him off, only to end up completely at odds with one another. But still, I feel a little angry.

We arrived in Minamata at around eleven o'clock, having managed to make our peace again on the train. A little up the slope near the station, along the Kagoshima Main Line, we spotted what appeared to be the old house of an illustrious family. Attached to it was a tranquil, luxuriant garden, with a mountain standing off to the back. We were intrigued, and after talking it over a bit, we decided to ask the family to let us see the house, knowing full well how rude we were being.

"We are from the naval air station in Izumi," we said, introducing ourselves. "And we were wondering—that is, if it's no inconvenience to you—if we might enjoy your garden while we take a rest." And they graciously ushered us in.

We found ourselves treated to a subtle infusion of powdered tea, which we rarely have a chance to drink, along with some cakes from Kagoshima called *harukoma*. The head of this household is a Mr. Nobunori Fukai. The family served the lords of Minamata Castle for generations. Mr. and Mrs. Fukai appear to be in their fifties, and they have a gentle, pleasant daughter, probably a few years younger than we are. She made the tea for us. There was a discreet garden pond among the bushes, and I could hear water dripping off the rocks. Deutzias were flowering. We grew silent for some reason, but we were fully gratified at heart. Personally, I have never been much interested in the gardens at Dai-sen-in or at Ryoan-ji Temple, and I certainly don't mean to compare the Fukais' garden with those. But it has been a very long time since I knew such serenity, and in such a peaceful setting.

As noon approached, they offered us a few tidbits. We declined, not wishing to abuse their hospitality, but they insisted. And after that, it was "Bread is better than birdsong," as they say. (I can't deny that we had more or less anticipated this.) Gratefully we enjoyed locally brewed sake, bonito sashimi garnished with ginger, sea urchin from Shimonoseki, and Suizenji seaweed soup, all the while telling the Fukais of our present circumstances and of our backgrounds. The Fukais have a son, a graduate of Keio University, who serves as a technical lieutenant in an army unit at

Tianjin. They said fate brought us together and expressed the hope that we would visit whenever we were given an outing, treating their home as our own. We took our leave at around one thirty, in high spirits—in fact, feeling blessed.

However, the meal the Fukais served was a bit too elegant to fill our stomachs, and when we returned to Izumi we ate a plate of fried rice with chicken, two bowls of *oyako-donburi*, a plate of sushi, and some scalloped noodles, and finally satisfied ourselves. As might be expected, I left more than half of my dinner at the base untouched. But I am becoming voracious again these days.

JUNE 15

American troops have started landing on Saipan. I heard that the combined fleet hoisted a "Z" flag and sailed in with all its remaining vessels. They haven't announced any military results yet.

We had our first takeoff and landing exercises. It was a dual flight and we all scrambled to get the good voice tubes. Wind direction: North. Wind velocity: Beaufort No. 7. I flew for thirty minutes.

The special course today was glider training. In bursts of fifty paces, done on the double, we hauled a secondary glider out to the end of the airfield. In the midst of the exercise, G.'s towline broke, injuring him slightly and snapping his watch band. The watch flew off into the air, and we searched for it after the order to cease the exercise was issued. It was a pleasure to grope about in the grass for the lost watch, teasing one another. "It's a treasure hunt at our seaside school," someone said. "Whoever finds the watch, he'll get G.'s milk tomorrow."

The day was long, and we cast deep shadows across the grass. I found myself more curious about the lark eggs nestled out here somewhere than about G.'s watch. I lay down flat so as to spot the bird when it alighted, and then made a search. After a few tries, I found the nest: three tiny eggs, gray-colored and oval-shaped, neatly arranged. The lark chattered on anxiously from a distance. M. told me that if a person touches its eggs, a bird will refuse to sit on them, so I gave it up, leaving the nest and my heart behind.

"Here it is!" someone shouted. The works of the watch were still intact and with a new glass cover it will be perfectly usable. We were all set to return to the barracks when Wakatsuki cried out abruptly, eyes skyward, "What the hell?!" We all looked up, and beheld an aircraft engaged in aerobatic exercises. A man had crawled out on its wing.

"Ack!" we gasped, as the body pulled away from the plane, plummeting, as if sucked down, over beyond the field headquarters, from an altitude of 800 meters. The man died instantly. It looks like a suicide. The plane went into a spin and crashed in a barley field. It wasn't long before his identity was disclosed: Senior Aviation Petty Officer D., an instructor attached to the 7th Division. I couldn't fathom it. Why, at such a crucial time, would he kill himself, wasting his valuable skills?

I asked Instructor Yamaguchi about it when he stopped by the barracks after dinner. "It was probably a woman," he replied matter-of-factly. But as to that, my mind wasn't settled, and in the evening I got poor marks during signal-communication drills. The transmission speed is fifty-five letters per minute. From the OD's room, the instructor sent in all manner of playful messages.

"Haveyoufoundlarkeggs?"

"Yesterdayastudentsnuckintothekitchentocabbagesugar Iknowwhodiditbutwon'ttellthesseniorofficersDestroythismessag ewhenyougetit." (Those who got it laughed.)

"Raiseyourhandifyougetthefollowingabbreviations."

"*hoshiyohoshi*." (This means "from gunner to gunner.")

"*kayotsushi*." ("from captain to signaler.")

"*totototo*." ("make an all-out charge"—a signal we will doubtless use some day.)

They made the rounds at 2130. Senior Aviation Petty Officer D.'s suicide left me dismayed.

JUNE 28

In the morning, the chief flight officer gave us a lesson on torpedo tactics in the drill hall. But whatever the topic (navigation, torpedoes, etc.) it is all basically a review of what we learned at Tsuchiura. This officer doesn't appear to be comfortable in the classroom anyway, and his talk grew livelier when he turned to the military situation on Saipan.

The newspapers all say, "Our women bravely rise up! Reenactment of the Mongolian Invasions at Iki Island!" But it seems the hostile troops have already seized a good portion of the island. Should Saipan fall, all the bases north of the South Sea Islands, such as those on Tinian, Iwo-jima, Guam, and Truk, will likely be useless, and the enemy will advance full clip toward the Philippines and mainland Japan. We have yielded control of the skies, and the enemy task force cruises freely around the Marianas. I hear that the combined fleet lost three of its jewels—the aircraft carriers *Taiho, Shokaku,* and *Hiyo*—and that it has already left the theater of operations, fleeing to a point not so very far from where we sit behind the scenes. The enemy fleet has emerged more or less unscathed, they say. It's distressing to think that this operation degenerated into yet another lost battle. Japan must retain some kind of confidence in her future success, but it's all so mortifying. I can't bear to sit on my hands back here. Sometimes I fear we might not complete our training in time. But even as I say this, the thought steals into my mind that I might actually return home alive. I banish this idea as best I can, partly because we are forbidden to entertain it, but mostly because I know I will lose my edge in the cockpit if I ever allow it to take root, and this would be dangerous. There is no denying that the grim complexion of the war unsettles me, though. I am also, to some degree, affected by Fujikura's opinions.

Flight training this afternoon, as the sky cleared up. They say the better trainees will be allowed to fly solo before long. I guess I'm making some sort of progress, but I had a stomach problem for three days, coinciding more or less with the naval battle in the Marianas. I brought up three large basins of vomit, so exhausting myself that I had to take a few days off, and thus I've fallen behind. I feel very questionable.

Today I was assigned the duty of recording secretary. I attended the division officer at field headquarters, clipboard in hand, and timed each flight from takeoff to landing.

"Aircraft #X taking off."

"The wind has shifted."

"Aircraft #Y, you are not clear for takeoff."

"'Gyro' requests permission to land."

"'Gyro' may land."

"'Deck' will now land."

On and on it went. It was quite nerve-wracking.

Wakatsuki suffered an accident. His plane (#4) flipped when its landing gear hung up on an obstruction during landing, and he ground to a halt upside down. I held my breath. We wear seatbelts and shoulder straps to bind us into the airplane, but in due course Wakatsuki untangled himself and emerged unperturbed with the instructor. God bless the Red Dragonfly! Had it been a real warplane, they would have both been goners. The Red Dragonflies are very stable. If we ever lose control in the air, they tell us, we should simply let go of the stick, and the plane will right itself naturally. Wakatsuki had a slight limp. But nevertheless he managed to sprint to the command tent and shout out a report, his face flushed, "Aircraft #4, Cadet Wakatsuki, reporting in from the third flight! The landing gear was damaged, and the propeller was completely destroyed! There is no other problem!"

The division officer motioned Wakatsuki forward until they stood face to face, then he gave him a whack. "Idiot! You sound like you're proud! You damaged the undercarriage. You wrecked the propeller. And there is *no* other problem?"

Relieved of my recording duty, I climbed into aircraft #7 for her eighth flight of the day. After taking off, I penetrated the clouds at an altitude of 300 meters. I call them clouds, but they were wispy, more like mist really. They slipped by at tremendous speed. The airfield vanished and then reappeared through the rifts. The island mountains of Amakusa were draped in clouds. The scene brought back a memory of a trip to Unzen I once made with my parents during the rainy season, when our bus climbed up through the mist.

All in all, the most difficult thing is to complete a pull-out at five meters as you come in to land. Unlike army pilots, navy fliers must execute a pullout-and-stall at a height of five meters in order to drop the tail of the plane for a three-point landing on the deck of an aircraft carrier. No matter how many times I try, I wind up touching down front-wheel first. I need more experience if I am ever to get the hang of it.

Flight operations exhaust me. I crave for books during our evening study sessions. Strange to say, though, these days I don't ever feel like taking up the *Manyoshu*. Stray poems from it come to mind during breaks between lectures and flight training, but I feel no inclination to open up the book and read. Instead, I want to read someone who can school a young fighter on matters of real consequence, firmly but responsibly, and in light of our actual situation. But such books are few and far between. Otherwise, I prefer to read something short and sweet, say, the fairy tales of Andersen, or the stories of Chekhov. Some men attain self-forgetfulness through the pleasures of the table, but only one thing really eases my mind: reading a great book that admits me to a wonderfully secure world. I will write home for a few.

JULY 8

Yesterday was the night of the Star Festival. We stood in ranks facing the moon and practiced issuing commands. The Milky Way was beautiful.

The Star Festival puts me in mind of the girls in the merchants' district of Osaka. Dolled up in large-patterned red *yukata* and yellow waistbands, they sit outside on benches, fans in hand, and chat idly along in their regional accent.

"That's not right, Yuki-chan. That's just not fair."
"Yeah, but my brother said it's okay."

The sweet colloquial rhythms of Osaka echoing in my ears, before my eyes a slip of silver paper inscribed with the words "Star Festival," the glow of sparklers. . . . But soon enough we are placed on Defense Condition 1. No time to fantasize about girls in *yukata*. It would appear that better than a dozen B-29s flew in from the direction of Chengdu, China, for a midnight raid on northern and western Kyushu. Yahata, Sasebo, and other cities all suffered damage.

Today is Imperial Rescript Day. The Sunday schedule was unexpectedly applied, and we were granted liberty. We took the train to Minamata and headed straight for the Fukais. Mr. Fukai was in Kumamoto today. The daughter, Fukiko, helped her mother prepare a meal for us, wearing pants made from a coarse, splash-patterned fabric. I felt guilty barging in unannounced. But what might otherwise have been a plain-looking pair of work pants looked fetching on Fukiko. The subdued light of the Fukais' house imparted a grace to her fair face and limbs, and I have never known a girl with such elegant nails. Mrs. Fukai kept us company for the most part, while Fukiko, to our disappointment, tended to disappear into the kitchen, not that any of us (I assume) was thinking of her in any special way. We aren't allowed to indulge such thoughts. Fukiko is quiet by nature, but she laughed with amusement when we related the story of Wakatsuki emerging from his plane so free of care after landing it upside down.

I learned for the first time that Tokutomi Roka was from Minamata. The Fukais have a number of old books of essays by local literary figures, and also a volume called the *Ashikita County Chronicle*, which compiles folk songs, ballads, and legends.

I found a few interesting hulling songs: "Long may my old man live, until the fire bell at the temple rots." "Divert yourself with song, instead of crying about your work." And a horse driver's chant: "If you sing as you please, the trees and reeds will nod, and the river stop to listen."

I suggested that we visit the Fukais whenever we are granted an outing, and that each time we copy out a few of these old folk poems, with a view toward making a notebook.

"Sure. Sounds interesting. Let's do it," Sakai agreed.

Fujikura, however, was displeased. "This isn't a Japanese Lit class," he said. "Stop your masturbatory trifling, and don't be so mawkish." He seems to be in the habit of objecting on principle to whatever it is we propose.

For dessert we were served a sweet soup of parched barley flour with dumplings. I stirred the barley flour into the boiling water and raised the bowl to my mouth, savoring its clean bucolic flavor, its gentle aroma and warmth. It was pure delight.

We returned to base at 1630. Tonight we learned that the final charge was in progress on Saipan.

JULY 18

First solo flight today. Intense heat, glaring sun, blue sky, and cumulonimbus clouds.

The men on Saipan died honorably, I heard. In the early morning of July 7, they launched their final all-out assault.

Some managed to steer in close to Mt. Tapotchau, inflicting heavy losses on the enemy, but all are believed to have met their heroic deaths no later than the 16th. Vice Admiral Chuichi Nagumo, task force leader at the Battle of Hawaii, was also killed in action.

"Ours is not to reason why, ours is but to do or die." We may fall, or we may kick in hard, but we must do it all without question, and that is our life.

I scarcely have time even to write this.

JULY 31

I was permitted to fly solo only the other day, and now I am already training in aerobatics.

The summer sea and clouds are exceptionally beautiful. From an altitude of 1200 meters, I made a nosedive toward a fishing boat, a solitary dot on the sea. I made a loop and executed a hammer-head stall and a vertical turn. Up in the sky the air is cool and pleasant, and aerobatic flying is a thrill, but it seems that the brain works far less efficiently at high altitude. Besides, I feel lousy all day after a flight, and my head grows heavy, as if it were under pressure.

Still, since we began aerobatics and formation flight training, I have noticed on the faces of my comrades the serene expression of men who act without worry about the outcome, as well as a few menacing looks. Flying demands the most rigorous attention, a kind of total effort. At all other times, there is just no use thinking about anything. My body perpetually craves watermelon, cold drinks, and the like.

They conducted a survey as to which type of aircraft we wish to fly. I listed carrier-based attack bombers for my first choice, land-based attack bombers for my second. In short, I have decided to fly hugging a torpedo to my belly. After all, if we don't do it, nobody will. Enemy troops have landed on Guam, and they have also reached Palau. Dalian reportedly suffered an air raid last night. The 1st Division and the 8th Division start night-flight training tomorrow. In fact, night-flight training is the ultimate course. We have come a long way in short order. Prepare for death with composure.

A letter from father arrived today, together with Mokichi Saito's *Winter Clouds* and the Iwanami paperback of Chekhov's stories. They still know nothing of my brother Bunkichi's whereabouts, and, as news comes in of suicidal charges made on one island after another, they worry, ominously.

When I open *Winter Clouds*, the poems about battles, and about Yamato, naturally seize my heart. However, the poems collected here date from 1937 to 1939, which means Saito's sentiment is often rather distant from ours, even if he does speak of war.

> When a nation rises,
> When her spirit tops the brim,
> Her sons find their peace
> Even in death.

> My heart full
> With news of battles won,
> I greet the New Year:
> My mind like still water.

BURIAL IN THE CLOUDS

If I put out to sea
I shall become a water-soaked corpse:
The guns roar in felicitation
Over the Pacific.

Given the present complexion of the war, I could never
express such wholehearted "felicitations." I will copy down a few
other poems that caught my eye.

A white blanket of snow
Covers the mountains peak to foot:
All buried, the houses and villages,
In retreat.
(This is a prefatory poem.)

The Japanese cemetery at Singapore.
As I wandered about
Tears brimmed in my eyes:
That memory came to mind.

In the rains falling round me
Where I stand still
Celestial Mt. Kagu-yama,
Now shrouded in mist.

This longing to see the weir
At the old capitol of Fujiwara:
Already my straw sandals are soaking wet.

They refuse to wear parachutes,
These air-raiders,
Saluting as they prepare for takeoff.

One after another, yesterday and today,
My friends ship out for the front,
Leaving my heart wild.

I can but stare
At this newspaper report:
A family has sent out five conscripts.

"The Pacific"
Sailing out onto this ocean:
You meet waves sky-high,
You find a sea of oily smoothness.

Saito wrote a couple of poems celebrating the wedding of Yoshiko Nakamura (probably the daughter of the late Kenkichi Nakamura).

What a lovely young couple:
As you drift off to sleep tonight,
This life, this world,
All of it shall look sublime.

Such a joyous occasion:
As she sits, sentiments well up,
Wave upon wave,
And overflow as tears.

In all likelihood I will die before ever having this experience.

I haven't been able to finish the book yet, but for the first time in a long while, I actually enjoyed reading poetry.

Excursion today. We ventured in a new direction, heading out to Akune. The hot springs there are very salty, as the water flows across a bed of halite before gushing out. My body felt sticky. Still, we bathed after taking a rest, and bathed yet again after lunch, making the most of it. The Chinese poet Bai Juyi writes, "The smooth hot spring water laved her creamy skin." In our case, it just wrung all the sweat from our bodies. But to men living in such times, to men situated as we are, a hot spring welling up so inexhaustibly, so mysteriously, by day and by night, seems a natural benediction.

It's sweltering. Not a drop of rain for the last ten days or so. I saw a rice field from the train, cracked by the sun. At the inn, the greenness of the garden was oppressive, and large brown cicadas chirred, intensifying the heat. The fried tiger prawns were delicious, and I ended up ordering three helpings. The watermelon was ripe and sweet. There was only one fly in the ointment: The beer wasn't cold enough, probably due to the shortage of ice.

We checked the train schedule only to discover that we hadn't time to go to Minamata today, though the Fukais might well have expected us, so we headed straight back to the base. Oleander bloomed here and there (sumac and oleander are ubiquitous in these parts). Oleander flowers are lovely, but a stranger on the train told us that the tree is toxic. During the Seinan War, the government soldiers ate lunch using oleander twigs for chopsticks, and many were poisoned. We also learned that this region is renowned as the migratory home of cranes. Flocks of hooded cranes fly in from Siberia every winter.

When we returned, two postcards awaited me, one from Professor E., the other from Kashima. To my surprise, Kashima has been in Kyushu since last month. The address read: "Yoshihiko Kashima, 120th Outfit, Provisional Torpedo Boat Training Camp, Kawatana-machi, Nagasaki Prefecture." This is a special camp where men train in high-speed torpedo boats, lightweight crafts made of plywood and fitted out with aircraft engines. Their purpose is to launch close-quarter torpedo attacks on enemy warships.

"You guys come in from the air," Kashima wrote, "I will come in on the water, and A. will creep in over the earth. Let's keep up the work." "A." is A.K. of Oriental History, and a high school classmate of Kashima. Apparently he has been sent to Naval Gunnery School at Tateyama. "I don't know which way Izumi is," Kashima continued, and then he adapted a poem from the *Manyoshu*: "'If I forget how you look / I shall call you to mind / When I look at the clouds / That cover the plain and rise / Up to the mountaintop.' Har har." Well, he could look Izumi up on a map.

Professor E. is serving fifteen-day stints at Toyokawa Naval Arsenal in Aichi Prefecture, leading students from the faculties of Law, Letters, and Economics. Since the emergency Student Mobilization Order was issued, academic work has been virtually suspended at the university.

"I have much to say about my experience in Toyokawa," the professor writes. "I just can't say it on a postcard." I can imagine the general situation.

Sunny today. The cool rush of the night air tells me that autumn is approaching, and in this hint of a changing season I also feel the creeping shadow of death. From the window of the barracks, I see the clear sickle of the crescent moon.

For some time now I have neglected to keep my diary. When we were in Tsuchiura, the division officer gave us a bit of advice: "You are free to keep a diary," he said, "but its contents may be private, and since navy fliers must rely on others to see to their personal effects if they are killed, it is best, so far as you can manage it, never to write anything that might tarnish your name after death." At the time, this gave me a little start, but lately I don't much care whether or not my name is tarnished after I die. I don't say this with any special conviction, as if I had resolved to take my own path and leave it to survivors to judge my life. On the contrary, I'm probably just backsliding. Well, in a word, I just don't give a damn.

As my mind grew passive, keeping a diary came to seem a pathetic exercise in literary masturbation, the sole outlet of my posthumous vanity. After all, I'm conscious of my readers as I compose. I play the scholar in front of my navy instructors and comrades, and I play the manly naval aviation student reserve officer in front of my university professors and parents, but really it's all nothing except lies rolled up in grumbles. These thoughts occupied me, and I didn't have the heart to take up a pen. In fact, I have eighty seven hundred sixty hours left, if I'm to live out another year, and I don't really see the point in setting aside some portion of my limited time in order to write this tripe. And yet when I abandoned what had become a custom with me—writing in my diary during our nightly study sessions—I was overcome with the feeling that something was missing, just as you might feel the need to put something in your mouth after quitting smoking. So today I am inclined to start writing again, and if it's masturbation, then so be it.

I might be on the verge of a nervous breakdown. Sometimes I feel utterly lost. I know nothing about keeping a diary, nothing about the war, nothing about life, nothing about death, nothing about scholarship either. I'm just a vacillator. What on earth is there in me that can be "tarnished" after I am gone? I notched up my petty successes, with self-satisfaction, from junior high to high school, from high school to university, and I left the university to become a pilot in the Navy Air Corps, fancying myself as "honorably" singled out. I can't resist the feeling that I am being stripped bare, so that I might see what my life really amounts to in the end. Not that I can handle an airplane better than anyone else, or that I can face my death with resolution. At the end of the day, I suppose, I simply have no core. I can't even compose a single satisfactory *tanka*, even under such uniquely tumultuous circumstances as these.

To my vexation, by and large I am in accord with what I am told, but none of it ever catches fire inside me. I can only conclude that I don't have what it takes, that I'm not numbered among those who burn with zeal. I am instructed to purify my mind of worldly thoughts, but what will become of me if I struggle, again and again, to detach myself and still fail, if I am committed utterly to the task and still cannot emancipate myself from what entangles me? Fortunately, during flight my brain functions only at about one-third of its natural capacity. It would be disastrous if thoughts like these swept over me in the cockpit. When, two months back, Senior Aviation Petty Officer D. leapt from the wing of his plane to his death, Instructor Yamaguchi chalked it up to a woman, and the explanation half convinced me. But now I wonder if his case might not have been so simple. Should my skill ever reach such a level as to free my mind up to wander while I fly, I can well imagine that my hand may, of its own accord, shove the control stick forward, sending the plane into a nosedive. I would kill myself, hardly even aware that I was to die. This is certainly among the possibilities, and if it should happen, the men will cremate my body, hold a wake by my ashes, and then forget about me as they return to their affairs, just as we all did when Senior Aviation Petty Officer D. perished. These men are strong; they possess the tenacity of an insect.

What's more, I believe that I am unduly influenced by Fujikura, even as I oppose him. My nervous breakdown might well be called "Fujikura's neurasthenia." When, on occasion, I find myself in good spirits, possessed of a forthright warrior's disposition, Fujikura's voice inevitably intrudes upon me. Of course, he sometimes does come and talk to me in person, but for the most part, it is his words—what he has said and is likely to say—that haunt me, shattering my resolve.

"'A forthright warrior's disposition'? What does *that* mean?"

"Doesn't it ever occur to you to doubt a war that militarists, capitalists, and politicians started on a gamble? Do you really consider it an honor to sacrifice your life in such a war?"

"No, you don't really believe it. You're just obsessed with the notion and too scared to question it."

"Why don't you take a good hard look, a *patient* look, at your innermost self, and at the condition of the war?"

And I offer my weak reply, closing my eyes. "Yes, I understand. I understand what you're saying."

Then an instructor's voice displaces Fujikura's. "What's eating you, Cadet Yoshino?" And not one of those bitter old maids who hang on in the training units, but my favorite instructor, the gentle, plain-spoken, clear-eyed chief flight officer whom we all call "the long-nosed goblin of Kurama." "You look depressed," he says. "Open your eyes and examine the situation. Things have come to such a pass that no one can say the tragedy in Saipan won't be repeated scene for scene on mainland Japan. If we don't want to see our country destroyed, we have to pitch in hard. We have no alternative. I know it's difficult, but you must follow me without qualms. You can't grip the control stick while casting a backward glance."

"I understand, sir," I reply, snapping to attention in my daydream. Can there be such a spineless attack bomber pilot as I am, a man who understands a little of this and a little of that, a man who is half-assed in everything?

My energy drains away into fancies of an old hermit's life (and here I am, a mere twenty-four years of age!), and then the reverie absorbs me utterly. . . . *Alongside a mountain stream, deep in the hills and bathed by the sun, there stands a forlorn cottage. Bestowed with the blessings of birdsong and abundant fruit, and with a few books to read and a good country wife to talk to, I will consign my feckless self to the vicissitudes of nature, like the grasses that grow silently and wither silently, locking all the old agitations away in my heart, and close my life in solitude and peace. . . .* At other times I summon up as my ideal something rather more concrete. In this scenario, I'm pushing along a wheelbarrow full of tomatoes on a farm of my own, or capering about with puppyish children at a district school, on some small island of terraced fields. . . . But then the whistle sounds beyond the deck, "*Hoa-hi-hoa*! Cease work in five minutes," and I pull out of my stupor.

Speaking of Saipan, I heard the following tale from a PO in the mess hall. The POs there are generally a realistic, hedonistic lot, fat and flabby—not at all the "gallant" type. Anyhow, this officer said that on a small island off Guadalcanal two navy signalers, men who had been left behind all but dead, somehow managed to filch a canoe and make their escape. Open wounds festered on their legs, streaming with bloody pus, and they had nothing at all to eat. For several days they drifted with the tide, gnawing their leather belts. Finally they made shore on a strange island. Human voices were audible just beyond a cliff draped with grasses and tree branches. The men couldn't tell whether the voices belonged to friend or to foe, but still they ventured to land. It turned out to be a Japanese army unit, and the two signalers were safely packed off to Saipan. From there, one of them was shipped back to Yokosuka, but the other, whose infection was not so severe, stayed on at Saipan, and when his health recovered, he was assigned to the island's signal unit. On the fortieth day after his rescue the American troops started landing, and this signaler, aware now that he would not survive, despite having made such a harrowing escape, rapped out a message in plain language to all navy units as he went to his death: "Damn the Imperial Navy."

"It might be true," the PO said. I just don't know how credible the story is.

We hear of three successive uprisings in Korea recently. Once I might have dismissed the rioters as a nuisance, but now I believe their actions may spring from a perfectly natural impulse. Japan talks about a lasting peace in East Asia, a peace on whose terms every nation can agree, but Japan has never said she will grant Korea her independence. What could be more reasonable than that Koreans should resent being asked to bow at shrines consecrated to the Japanese dead? No wonder they don't share our concerns as to the outcome of the war, no wonder they resist conscription in a war that promises them no future. As for me, my fighting spirit burns when I recall the abuses that America, Britain, and all the other so-called "industrial" nations of the West have committed all over Asia for a hundred years, but I've rather indifferently tolerated our own nation's actions in China and Korea. At the time of my birth, Korea was already our possession, and we have harbored no doubts about it, but apparently the question is not so simple. I understand why the Koreans believe they will be liberated should Japan lose this war, and if, capitalizing on Japan's deteriorating military position, they take to the streets rather than be drafted before that day of liberation comes, I can understand that, too. Perhaps my weak heart sympathizes with a weak and oppressed people. I have no idea whether that is a good thing or a bad thing.

AUGUST 26

Insects sing constantly, and it's quite cool, morning and evening. The tadpoles that once swarmed in the gutters at the barracks vanished before I noticed. My heart sinks deep, deep as it ever has. I received a severe reprimand from the division officer.

The fledgling sparrows, now barely able to fly, leap in flurries from the gutters to the eaves of the panoptic auditorium. The lecture on the science of war fades from view as I watch them, vacantly. Timidly the siblings launch desperately into flight. Nevertheless, they fly in order to live.

We are allowed considerable freedom now during solo flights, so I flew over Minamata the other day, where I could easily make out the Fukais' place. The lines of the earthen wall enclosing it to the southwest looked lovely from the air. I dove twice in salutation. Neither Fukiko nor anybody else came out, though I flew so close to the ground that the roar of the plane shook the pine tree in the garden. It was a disappointment. In a field, children threw up their arms at me. I replied with a waggle of the wings and headed back. I wasn't upbraided for any of this, as they didn't find out about it, but today I flew out to sea and spotted a fleet of ships steaming along some twelve nautical miles south-southwest of Ushibuka, a town on the main island of Amakusa. The fleet consisted of an enormous battleship, escorted by two destroyers and two heavy cruisers. The ships dominated the seascape, leaving behind them five snowy wakes as they cruised over rough blue waters ruffled with whitecaps. Stirred by a tender pride, I set a course for the battleship, and, at an altitude 700 meters, whizzed by. No sooner had I passed over the ship, however, than her antiaircraft machine guns and high-angle canon opened up on me simultaneously, emitting sharp flashes of light. I was stunned and wheeled about in haste. At first I thought they mistook me for an enemy aircraft, but then I realized that they had in fact been firing blanks. I couldn't figure out why they opened fire, though, and could only conclude that I had inadvertently served as a target for antiaircraft fire training. As soon as I landed at Izumi, I was called in by the division officer.

"Where in the hell did you fly!?" he thundered, glaring at me. The battleship had been none other than the *Musashi,* as it happened, and he had already received a dispatch from its LC: "At 1025 a training aircraft from your base overflew this ship without permission, turned, and headed back. I request that you attend to the matter." I was fairly boiled in oil. I felt pathetic. This is precisely why you should never doze off during lectures on navy rules and regulations. I hadn't known we are forbidden to pass over a fleet of ships without permission.

SEPTEMBER 1

We conducted a mutual flight in formation.

I flew plane #2. Only the lead plane was piloted by an instructor. At one point I recklessly pulled in so close to him that my wing might easily have touched his. I held the position for several minutes. If we crash, I thought, then so be it. The lead plane would surely have gone down had we collided, as its tail assembly would have been damaged. We, however, would have likely survived, if it were just a matter of our plowing the propeller into the other plane. The crew in the lead plane was evidently anxious, as they glanced back at us constantly. But I didn't expect a scolding, because our instructions had been to "follow with a vengeance." Cowardly Sakai, in plane #3, fell off to the rear left, now and then, marring the formation. Perceiving this, the instructor lowered his altitude and banked left at a steep angle. As the umbrella formation suddenly inclined, Sakai, had he remained where he was, would have had no choice but to plunge into the sea. So he scrambled to catch up. It's a brutal, unforgiving tactic.

All goes like clockwork if I position my plane by keeping my body exactly between the rising sun painted on the fuselage of the lead plane and its main wing joint. When I'm flying over the ocean in tight formation, my hands and feet work fluidly, as if without any effort, and it feels good. The landing went off flawlessly, and as I pulled on to the apron, the command came to cease and return to the hangars. We taxied our airplanes in, gunning the throttles.

An armada of Ginga bombers attached to the Todoroki Unit advanced to this air station today. I have seen the Ginga before, at Tsuchiura. A top-secret prototype of this land-based bomber had been in development for years under the name "Y20," and I assume they finally managed to put it into mass production. Anyhow, I have never before seen a whole fleet of Gingas, and so close up, as well. The navy threw all its aeronautical science and technology into this plane. They say that the men who saw the first working prototype cried out in wonder at the sight of its elegant form. And it is indeed a refined, smartlooking aircraft. Its all-up weight is ten tons, which is heavier than the Type-1 land-based attack bombers, but in the air it is nimble.

The Todoroki crews took their lunch behind the array of Gingas, and, without so much as setting foot in the barracks, began training in the evening. They kept up their torpedo drills, and their navigation, communication, and dive-bombing drills, until about eleven o'clock at night. The roar was so deafening we could hardly hear what the duty officer said as he made his rounds. An ensign, from the 13th Student Reserves, strutted in with news of our advanced new aircraft—the carrier-based reconnaissance plane Saiun, the land-based patrol plane Tokai, the night fighter Gekko, and so on. All of which appears to have eased my nervous breakdown a little. As we listened, mightily impressed, this ensign of the 13th Student Reserves swelled with pride, carrying on for all the world as if he had himself built the Ginga, the Saiun, and everything else.

I heard from my mother. She said our figs are already ripe. That very day she had laid the first of them out in meals set for me and my brother Bunkichi, but where on earth is Bunkichi now? He might possibly have been killed on Saipan or some other such place, I vaguely thought.

SEPTEMBER 8

Red Dragonflies sank down onto the vast sward of green grass, one after another. Off behind a hazy island mountain, over across the sea of Shiranui, the sun was setting. I sat down and caught a whiff of the thick grass, now better than a foot in height. Insects sang riotously.

I gazed at the landscape, my legs in my arms. Once the sun slipped over the horizon, the mountain peaks of Amakusa showed their stark blackish silhouettes in the afterglow. The landing-light arrays burned in clear flames on the grass of the airfield. The weeds stand at eye level now, and they swayed in the breeze, intermittently obscuring the red flares from view. "If his father or his son falls in the battle, a warrior will gallop over the corpse and press the fight." So says *The Tale of the Heike* of the eastern samurai. I mustn't waver. I have no alternative but to become a gear in the machine, and I cannot yield to self-pity, but even as I say this, wayward feelings arise. I don't know what to do with them.

This morning a Ginga crashed right after taking off. Engine failure brought it down. I was attending a lecture on instrument flight, when, all of a sudden, black smoke plumed up in the direction of the administration building. I ran from the classroom and saw it: the Ginga burning like fury, blazing in black-red flames, just off to the front of the gate. I simply gazed at it, struck dumb by such an astounding sight. A real warplane is spectacular even in ruins. Through the smoke, I caught glimpses of the charred wing. I knew full well that three men were being immolated in that plane, but to my surprise, I felt almost nothing. As for the Todoroki Unit, nonchalant about it all, they lost no time in resuming operations, even as black smoke scorched the sky. We, too, returned to our classroom in fairly short order to continue our lecture on instrument flight.

I am told that the area around Izumi, particularly the islands of Katsura-jima and Nagashima, off Komenotsu, bears a strong resemblance to Pearl Harbor, both in its geographic features and its ocean currents. It may be just a local boast, but they say that, before the war started, the combined fleet conducted secret training exercises here for its surprise maneuver, and, therefore, that we owe our one-sided victory at Oahu to this place. But it now appears that our very success at Pearl Harbor did Japan a disservice. For one thing, it united the whole of America with a slogan: "Remember Pearl Harbor." For another, it encouraged a tendency in the navy to throw its weight around without really knowing its abilities. So much for the so-called "silent navy." The newspapers rave, frothing with shopworn phrases like "Mow them down!" "Search and destroy!" "British and American devils!" and so forth, all of which, lo and behold, the navy's central command incites. I suppose we had best replace the epithet "silent navy" with "chattering navy." In point of fact, we are subject now to a rough and risky regime in our training, due largely to the deteriorating quality of the fuel, with its interfusion of alcohol, and now even *that* fuel is scarce. They say we will have to temporarily discontinue flying the interme- diate trainers. Who can understand how a flier feels, held in such agonizing suspension?

The solid navy tradition is now a hollow shell. It holds to all the old patterns, but the spirit is gone. Is it any wonder if I criticize the Imperial Navy in its current incarnation? For example, we are specifically instructed to learn all necessary skills from the drill instructors, but never to associate with them in a personal way. Now, let's say that the deck officers from the Naval Academy are white men. Well, they treat the enlisted ranks just like black slaves, and as for the student reserves and reserve officers—they regard us with the diffident suspicion that white men reserve for the "yellow" race. It is all so conventional, so aristocratic. There were times when I thought we must ourselves become infected with this attitude if we were to succeed as naval officers. But now I can't help but consider it a bad case of Anglophilia. What could we possibly gain by deliberately opening up such chasms between the men? Anyway, in times like these we simply don't have the luxury to go out sporting pure white collars.

A man from Kyoto visited today, with reports that they are suffering severe shortages of supplies. A student had gone out to meet him, expecting a gift of sweets or something, but as it turned out, *he* ended up offering food to the man from Kyoto. What a disappointment! He watched as the man wolfed it all down, saying, "It sure would be swell to be in the navy. Surely it would be." Professor O. must be having a hard time getting his hands on his favorite Japanese confections.

SEPTEMBER 17, MEMORIAL DAY FOR THE
BATTLE OF THE YELLOW SEA

A typhoon has been approaching Kyushu since yesterday. With it come occasional bursts of rain. The barracks sprang a leak in the middle of the night, and we had to shift things around. Consequently, I didn't get enough sleep.

A ceremony was held from 0745 on the first floor of the barracks, after which we sang martial songs written for the Battle of the Yellow Sea: "The Brave Fight of the Akagi," "Audacious Sailors," and so on. Afterwards, we were granted liberty.

We heard that the Kagoshima Main Line was blocked off around Hinagu, but the usual three of us managed our excursion to Minamata anyway. However, the train schedule made for a hectic visit. We arrived at the Fukais' house at eleven and had to leave at half past one. It was as if we went there solely to eat lunch. Mrs. Fukai and Fukiko had to hustle to prepare a meal in time. Fukiko donned her rain gear and went out into the downpour to fetch something they needed, ignoring our pleas.

Today we were served *satsuma-imo*. As the name indicates, this region is the home of these yams, and they are certainly delicious, fluffy in texture, rather like chestnuts in taste, and not at all stringy. A package had arrived from Sakai's family in care of the Fukais, and it contained dried chestnuts and pancakes. To our regret, the pancakes were moldy, but, after carefully wiping them off, we savored them nonetheless. They weren't at all bad.

I told Fukiko about how, a while back, I paid my respects to the family during a training flight.

Fujikura broke in. "You did? So did I. I flew by during solo exercises just the other day. I could make out the stripes on Fukiko's clothes quite clearly." He seemed to take it for granted that Fukiko had turned out when I flew over. My heart sank.

"What time did you come?" Fukiko asked me, casting her eyes up in an effort to remember. "It's a wonder I didn't notice. Had I gone off shopping? But if I was out, I should have noticed it all the more. What happened?" Again and again she said she was sorry.

"You shouldn't be sorry." I laughed, but it seemed both accidental and somehow *not* accidental that she had heard the roar of Fujikura's plane and not the roar of mine. In any case, I wasn't really amused.

We returned to base in a slashing rainstorm. The rain cascaded over the windows of the train, and we couldn't so much as glimpse the scenery.

We haven't flown in more than a week, but at last the fuel has arrived. We should resume operations when the weather cooperates. Once we start flying again, and once our formation drills are complete, they will tell us which type of aircraft each of us is to pilot. Never shall I regret having requested assignment to a carrier-based attack bomber. I shall face the prospect with an open heart. There are only ten days to two weeks left of our life here at Izumi.

Another Ginga crashed yesterday. At about half past seven, the southwestern part of the already-darkened airfield suddenly flushed red, and a number of men from the Todoroki Unit sprinted off. I myself didn't go out to the site, but I was told that one Ginga, taking off at a speed of 80 knots, had plowed into another that was grounded for repairs. The reconnaissance crew and the signaler in the first plane died on the spot, and the pilot, who tumbled out engulfed in flames, was rushed off to the infirmary, out of which, at around ten o'clock at night, eight coffins emerged.

These days it is still dark at reveille, and there is a chill in the air. We do calisthenics after morning assembly, and as the alpenglow over Yahazutake Mountain diffuses across the eastern sky, taking on its tint of gold, one by one the black mountains shake off their sleep. And today, in the midst of such beauty, while we were engaged in calisthenics, outfitted all in white, as usual, three more coffins were borne from the infirmary. The toll of last night's accident is three crew members and eight mechanics, and the cause was carelessness. They say the Ginga is difficult to service. It costs eight hundred thousand yen to build one, and they struggle to produce eighty planes a month.

The majority of the Todoroki Unit, however, set out for Okinawa at 0930 today, leaving behind them, at this station, the souls of their comrades. They boarded the officers' bus in front of the administration building for their ride out to the airfield, and there they climbed into their planes, swords in hand, looking just as they do during daily training flights. "If you don't hear of any significant results in twenty days," this crew of the 13th Class told us, "then assume we have all been destroyed."

The signaler stood on the airplane waving a stick of some kind, and the Gingas lifted their tails and gallantly took off, one after another. The remaining forces of the Todoroki Unit, the student units, and everybody else drew up in columns along the runway and twirled their caps to see the men off. The Gingas flawlessly arrayed themselves in formation, took a course southward, and shortly disappeared from view.

As for us, we started instrument flying today. During the suspension of actual flights, we were trained quite well using a mock-up on the ground. This is a kind of aircraft-shaped box, into which we step, pulling down a curtain behind us. Only the control stick and the gauges are really lifelike, and as this motorized "airplane" quakes, we practice holding our position, solely by peering into a gauge. This is called "blind flight." And today we begin airborne instrument flight training.

We made a dual flight, instructor in the back, student in the front. A hood, only the back of which opens, is pulled down over the cockpit. The instructor does the takeoff and landing from the rear seat.

The command "Commence instrument flight" came in through the voice tube, and, with that, the stick was in my hands, at an altitude of one thousand meters exactly. Actually, it is quite difficult to fly blind. The needle on the gauge wiggles neurotically, and we must hold it in the correct and level position. I tend to the left. When the nose is up, the needle rises above the level line, and when the nose drops down, the needle plunges.

"You're going down! Watch out!" The scolding rang through the voice tube. I remember the experience well from the "dual" phase of formation flight training. The instructor, an aviation petty officer second class, would say, "What? Do you want to die!?" And availing himself of the elastic rubber voice tube, he would thwack my head from behind with its metal funnel. If that didn't do the trick, in came the order: "Release your hands and raise them." Well, it was no fun at all floating along in this *banzai* posture as a punishment. Thanks to the hood, I didn't have to do a *banzai* this time around, but I did have to keep a close eye on all the instruments—speedometer, altimeter, oil pressure indicator, thermometer—even while enduring a good dressing down. The flight lasted about thirty minutes. I gathered that most of the time we had been over the ocean, though, needless to say, I couldn't see anything at all.

When we completed our first round of instrument flights, the chief flight officer issued various instructions, and then he fell into a lament. The Army Air Corps, he says, lags far behind present-day aviation standards, and this is a problem. Army pilots know nothing of celestial navigation, and their instrument flight skills are dubious. Those who completed their course at Kagamiga-hara, in Gifu Prefecture, were instructed to make their "graduation" flight to Tokorozawa in Saitama. "Fly with Mt. Fuji on your left," they were told, "and you'll never get lost." And one of the pilots did exactly that. He kept on flying with Mt. Fuji on his left until he made seven circles around the mountain, ran out of fuel, and had to make an emergency landing. I trust we will never find ourselves in so undignified a predicament. Until recently, army pilots hadn't been capable of making the transoceanic flight from Kyushu to Formosa. Navy pilots had to escort them. Even so, by the time they reached Formosa, a number of army aircraft were missing in action. As the chief flight officer sees it, the Japanese military has served the nation badly, owing particularly to the "spiritualism," and to the smug disdain for technology, that is rampant in the army.

I was a bit more confident during the second instrument flight. This is our last course at Izumi. The time to graduate from the Red Dragonfly draws near, though; come to think of it, while flights were suspended during the fuel shortage, the familiar Red Dragonflies were all painted dark green.

SEPTEMBER 27

This is the last night I will ever sleep in the barracks at Izumi.

On the 22nd, I was told what type of aircraft I will fly. I have been assigned to carrier-based attack bombers and am to proceed to Usa. Fujikura drew the same assignment and the same posting. As for Sakai, he wavered toward carrier-based bombers after a Suisei, which flew through toward the end of last month, turned his head with its fancy maneuvers. He, too, is bound for Usa, to pilot a carrier-based bomber. The three of us must be linked up by some evil fate. Sixty-seven pilots for carrier-based attack bombers and forty-five for carrier-based bombers all ship out for Usa in the morning.

A rainbow arced across the evening sky today, but soon disappeared. It's a clear night with a bright moon. I can see the clouds in the dark sky. The barracks are seething, as the Matsushima-bound men leave tonight. So, it is farewell to Wakatsuki. Each of us knows that we will never see one another again, but all we say as we pass through the bustling hallways are things like "Hey, let's hit the bottle when next we meet." Everybody has a pleasant air and seems free of qualms. Loaned items have all been returned, and trunks are to be shipped out by truck. The men have little luggage. We shouldn't leave behind us too many personal belongings, too much homesickness, too much friendship.

We had a farewell party in the evening. We set desks out on the moonlit morning assembly ground, and each of us had smelly sashimi made from frozen fish, clear soup, red rice, two *ohagi* dappled with a little bean paste, and a bottle of beer. Still, we were elated and raised our voices in song—heart and soul. We tossed the chief flight officer, our long-nosed goblin of Kurama, up into the air.

Yesterday afternoon we made our valedictory flight. Our formation of twenty-seven planes approached Komenotsu from the direction of Akune. It was overcast and I couldn't see the mountains in the distance, but nevertheless it's so long, now, to the familiar sky where, on a clear day, I enjoyed a view of Sakura-jima at an altitude 600 meters, Takachiho at 1000, and Aso at 1500. It's also goodbye to the chimney of the Japan Nitrogen Company of Minamata, which I always used as a landmark. I flew comfortably in the #2 position in the first element of the first wing.

As it turned out, we managed to finish our courses here without a single accident. All the same, I myself almost caused two, just before our departure. The mishaps are more frightening to recall than they were to endure, because if I die now, I die absolutely in vain. The first took place on the day we got our assignments, during a "group" instrument flight, with D. manning the front seat. I sat in back and pulled down the hood. All went well in the air. I handed control of the plane over to D., saying, "End instrument flight." And, taking the hood into consideration as he prepared for landing, D. approached the strip at about sixty knots. But he misjudged our height when executing the "pullout." This should be done at five meters, but instead it seems D. pulled the control stick at around seven meters in altitude. As if that weren't enough, the stick was too responsive, and when he pulled it back halfway, we stalled at about four meters. And then we fell. My visibility was zero because of the hood, but I had been thinking we were too high. All of a sudden my body sank, and with a *bam*! came the impact, the aircraft touching down tail first, and then swirling to the left. We weren't hurt, but the left undercarriage of the trainer was fractured. The second incident occurred two days later. I was flying over the ocean when, at the horizon of my field of vision, where sea and sky met, I saw enormous billowing clouds sweeping to the side. They looked like a mountain chain rising up, or a massive cataract pouring into the cradle of the deep. I was reveling in the spectacle when, with absolutely no warning, my propeller stalled. Surely this was due to the fuel, adulterated as it is with alcohol. Instantly I broke out in a cold sweat and totally lost my composure. I managed none of the emergency measures we had been taught. Anyhow, I shifted into a nose-dive, whereupon the propeller started to crank, as if making sport of me.

We visited the Fukais the day before yesterday, to bid our farewell. They cooked red rice while awaiting our arrival. Even the carp in the pond wished us good luck on our departure, by becoming miso soup. I shall never forget the kindness of this family. We agreed that each of us would do one parlor trick. Sakai performed a card trick. Fujikura sang a silly song titled "Draw the Lamp and Catch the Lice," augmenting it with gestures. I did a vocal mimicry of a Bunraku puppet show called "East and West, East and West." Then all three of us sang "The Song of Trainee Pilots." Fukiko rose and disappeared, tears welling up in her eyes. But tears for whom? Well, it won't do to wonder. I must part gracefully.

It is ten forty-five now. "Those who are leaving this air station fall in in five minutes," comes the announcement from the loudspeaker. "All the rest of the students assemble for the send-off." So I take up my cap and go to see off the men bound for Matsushima.

Letter from Fujikura
Usa Naval Air Station, Oita Prefecture
October 5, Showa 19 (1944)
Yoshihiko Kashima
Provisional Torpedo Boat Training Camp,
Kawatana-machi, Nagasaki Prefecture

We moved here at the end of September. The station sits in the middle of a field near Usa Hachiman-gu Shrine, about an hour and a half train ride from Beppu. A river, which bears the odd name of Yakkan, runs nearby. So-called "military rules" and "moral orders" are stringently enforced. When we disembarked at Yanagiga-ura station, on the Nippo Main Line, three officers were there to meet us, oak bludgeons in their hands. "We're going to put you through the wringer. Prepare yourselves." That was their greeting. For a moment I thought we were here to join a gang. Since then, all slowpokes, and all who forget their salute, get beaten, one and all, every morning. It would appear that hits to the jaw fall under the rubric of "routine maintenance," and I get my maintenance at least three times a day. At night, I can hear, quite distinctly, the moans of the young trainees as those bullies put the screws to them. Do they actually believe they can arrest the fall of Japan with stunts like these?

Kashima, I know I haven't written you for a very long time. Still, I've been reading the cards you send to Yoshino and Sakai from time to time as they come in, and when was it that I noticed, since parting with you at Otake, that you had begun to deliver yourself of such brave sentiments so often in your letters?

"Let your *Manyoshu* pay tribute to me," you wrote. Now, did that really come from the bottom of your heart? I'm not being sarcastic, mind you. But I really would love to ask you how you could achieve such grace as that. The blunt fact of the matter is that I am immensely sad to see that even you have changed in this way.

Aren't these strange days? Politicians, military men, scholars, poets—all of them exhort us, *ad infinitum,* to eat potatoes and die with a smile. But not a word do they have about how we can survive to reconstruct Japan. Who on earth is giving any thought to the matter? I guess the *Manyoshu* wasn't quite the right subject to study, if we are aiming to face the world's political and economical developments with a level head, standing in the midst of these turbulent currents. I don't possess that order of confidence and ability. I simply object to this war because my instincts tell me to.

Before joining the navy at Otake, I sounded a number of people out for their opinions as to the outcome of this war. Only two predicted Japan would fail. One was a relative on my mother's side, a rear admiral back from the southern theater, and the other was a consumptive old upperclassman from my junior high school days who had been engaged in underground leftist activities. According to the rear admiral, an attempt to overthrow British and American hegemony in Asia, with Japan taking the lead, was inevitable, a historical necessity. But what did Japan do to accomplish that end? She misjudged the timing, indulged in all manner of self-righteous foolishness, and now it's indisputable: our defeat is a mathematical certainty. For his part, my junior high school buddy said his conviction that Japan would fall was rooted not in emotionalism and defeatism, but in scientific fact. And it was at that point that I became interested in both the navy and the Communist Party, odd though the combination may be. What these two men said is etched on my mind. Since joining the navy, however, I have grown weary of it. Nothing indicates to me now, in the present state of naval affairs, that the minority view can have any influence. Also, we were born a few years too late to take in any of the old leftist atmosphere in our campus life. Consequently we are anything but expert when it comes to Marxism. Had we been acquainted with the theory, even if we didn't accept it wholesale, I wonder whether or not we might have been able to adopt a more scientific perspective.

However, let's not split hairs. Maybe I'm just in a funk, but I simply can't see any reason why I should bottle it up. I don't want to die. I have no wish to sacrifice my life in this war. Kashima, why don't we do the best we can to survive? Each time he reads your manly letters, Yoshino swells up with martial spirit and fresh courage. Don't let's be too gallant.

What's your daily training like? The absolute minimum requirement for our survival is that we avoid accidents during our routine flight training. Since coming here, we have lost two men during orientation flights in the navy Type-97 carrier-based attack bomber. I think you remember O. (from Doshisha Univ.) and H. (from Hakodate Fisheries College), with whom we have been together since Otake. The instructor aboard the plane survived, though with serious injuries, but the two students perished. When we lower the flaps, the nose drops, and we must correct the bias with the trim tabs. It appears, however, that the pilot inadvertently reversed the tabs, and he couldn't pull out at an altitude of 200 meters. So the plane plunged into the sea, in a flash. I heard that the main wing was blown off when it hit the water. I was only two names away from this debacle on the flight roster. In the coffins, the men were adorned with the cherry-blossom insignia of ensign. It was a sad commission. Two students from Ryukoku University put vestments on over their military uniforms and read from the sutras. We held a wake for them all through the night, each member of the outfit taking a one-hour turn. They say the navy dislikes a quiet, solemn vigil, and that if the deceased loved to drink in life, well, then it should be "Bottoms up!" for a tribute. That's all well and good, but when it turned out that we needed to fetch another funeral wreath, in addition to what we already had on base, the deck petty officer said, keeping a straight face, "No problem. And why don't I get one more while I'm at it? We'll need it for the next time anyway." I was dumbfounded. We bore the dead off to a crematorium in Nakatsu today. We didn't let the bereaved families see them, as the bodies were quite discolored. The stoker at the crematorium was feeble from malnutrition, and he moved about listlessly; his heart wasn't in it. Very evidently he simply wished to be done with this task of setting the coffins ablaze. I was disgusted. But the parents, who had hurried all the way here, were too absentminded even to shed tears, and, in their apathy, they stood there looking like a regular bunch of stupid grown-ups. Maybe they couldn't believe the coffins actually contained their sons. And what did the instructor say when we returned to base? "Don't let one or two deaths dismay you. We'll put you through the wringer twice as hard, starting tomorrow."

Kashima, let's take the utmost care to make it through our training. Let's not earn the insignia of ensigns, or whatever, by dying. We can muddle along for the next several months, but then what will we do when we receive our commission, when we go into battle, when we make our sorties? No logic and no complaints will avail us then. I have known for quite some time that I will have to take measures, extreme measures, if I am to survive. I'm not yet at a point where I can say exactly how I am going to do this, not even to you. A thousand times the word "Coward!" crosses my mind, but I intend to banish it every time.

What I miss is the time I spent in Kyoto, as you might expect. I once expressed my gloomy feelings, and my nostalgia for Kyoto, in a long letter to Professor E., and received in return just another postcard of encouragement. I guess he had his reasons, but I had hardly written a letter of any kind before that, and since then I have been too discouraged to write to anyone again. I don't wish to place you under any obligation, or to make any demands. But I am wondering if you might reply to this letter. I'm going to post it from Beppu on our next day of liberty. If you reply, address

the letter to me "c/o Kajiya Inn, Kamegawa Hot Springs, Beppu."
Let me know the address you use on your outings, too.

So long, Kashima. Take care.

~⊃

Usa Naval Air Station

OCTOBER 13 (CONTINUED FROM YOSHINO'S DIARY)

The strict, taut atmosphere of this base is having a beneficial effect on my constitution, as before, what with all my backsliding, I had been on the verge of a nervous breakdown.

We rise five minutes prior to reveille, dash off to the airfield, and, in the predawn darkness, throw open the doors to the hangars. There, Type-97 carrier-based attack bombers—the same model that saw action in the Battle of Hawaii—await us, with their noses in alignment. Morning assembly follows, then naval calisthenics, then we're back to take the planes out, running every step of the way. It's bracing to see enlisted men salute us with such insistent rigor. We haul the planes out and extend the wings, consult the flight schedules, equip our seats with parachute, cushion, and voice tube, inspect the fuel, the oil, and the surface of the plane. All this accomplished, we feed our bodies on rice and hot miso soup, having worked up a pleasant hunger. Afterwards, we put on flight suits and sprint to the field.

Since arriving here, I am flush with a sense of well-being. I never sneeze. I think I have at last begun to internalize a spirit of enterprise, and it exhilarates me. Clearly this has a bearing on my physical health. Positive and negative aren't far apart; they are not the two extremes. And my complaints about the navy, my anxieties as to the war situation, my self-doubts— somehow I must integrate these into something forward-looking, into something redemptive.

The newspaper reports that carrier-based enemy aircraft raided Formosa from a mobile force consisting of almost the entire U.S. Pacific Fleet. If we are to recover, it will require no ordinary effort. Now is not the occasion to indulge ourselves in pointless grief over the martyrdom of O. and H. When we five thousand pilots of the 13th and 14th Student Reserves fly into the jaws of death, with some twenty thousand trainee pilots backing us up, for the first time there will be a decisive turn in the progress of this war.

I was reading a novel titled *Naval Battle* when I encountered the author's confession: "All along I have been searching for what might prepare me," he says, "as if it were a solid object." Exactly. But on the contrary, only what flows into your mind naturally, filling it up by accretion, can truly prepare you. Something in me rises like the tide, overwhelming my inner conflicts. I feel that now, and it is gratifying.

Today I made my fourth dual flight, practicing take-offs and landings in a Type-97. Altitude: 800 meters. As I sat in the back seat, turning round on the lookout, I got a sense of our speed. Much faster than the intermediate trainers we flew at Izumi. The propellers are metal, and the sound of the engine differs. The Type-97 is a low-wing monoplane with a high rate of climb. It gains altitude in an instant, making me realize that I'm in a truly first-class aircraft, an aircraft that has performed in battle. They say that in a fast plane you are already in your turn the instant you even *think* of turning. Indeed, the plane does respond to even the slightest shift of the control stick. Consequently, it's hard to get the hang of things. I'll have to learn how to get my bearings using the Type-97's sensitive altimeter, variometer, and longitudinal inclination indicator. The pullout at seven meters is easier to make in the Type-97 than in our intermediate trainers. Two out of three of our landings were just about picture perfect, which was satisfying. The trick, it would appear, is to pull the bar all the way in at the end.

Flights ceased at 1400. Afterwards, they issued each of us a ten-day supply of flight rations: one bottle of soda, six packets of cod liver oil, two parcels of high-altitude flight food, one parcel of chocolate, and a large can of pineapple. In addition, to each outfit of twelve pilots they distributed a gallon of orange wine, two bottles of tonic, two of orange syrup, two of lemon juice, one of coffee, and one of amazake. Laid out all together, it was quite a bounty. Everyone beamed. Still more, our meals are augmented with in-flight food at breakfast every morning, milk or an egg at lunch, one *ohagi*, hardtack, a glass of orange juice at dinner, and, every other night, a plate of maki-zushi. Who eats like this in the outside world these days? Well, why shouldn't I bestir myself?

OCTOBER 17

News of the results of the aerial battle over Formosa comes rolling in. Quite impressive. We sank eleven aircraft carriers and disabled three more. Two battleships went down, along with three cruisers and one destroyer. In total, we sent forty-odd ships to the bottom of the sea. The newspaper calls it the work of the gods, which I let stand without a murmur. Excellent work.

There is a story behind these remarkable results, though. No fewer than three hundred twelve of our warplanes failed to return from their sorties. Add to this those planes that were destroyed on the ground, and those that crash-landed, and you have a total of some seven or eight hundred aircraft lost. The estimate is that we also lost nearly a thousand aircrews. It would appear that our 2nd Air Fleet was essentially annihilated in exchange for our brilliant results. Most of the Gingas from the Todoroki Unit, the unit we spent some time with back at Izumi, must have been lost. Someday we will fight just as they did. My only wish is for a wise move now on the part of the operations section.

While the results of the battle were being announced this morning, two damaged carrier-based bombers emerged from the fog, buzzing the radio tower and making an emergency landing. On board were senior aviation petty officers who had taken part in the attacks of yesterday. They were flying inland from Formosa to retrieve fresh aircraft, but bad weather compelled them to land on our base.

According to these men, the enemy fleet is, at present, on the lam at five knots, and what's more, it has no fighter cover at all. If only we had the strength, they say, we could sweep the fleet away, but there are no planes left for the pursuit. Five knots is the speed of an ordinary boat. I couldn't be more exasperated. But these men didn't appear to be wired, and they mumbled when they spoke. Their eyes, however, smoldered with an uncanny menace.

In the evening, I picked up a postcard from Kashima in Kawatana. It had arrived with the afternoon mail.

"We haven't written each other in some time," it read. "Whenever I see an airplane I think of you all. And I had been longing for some word from you, even if only about pampas grass swaying in the breeze or a sparrow singing, when a long letter came in yesterday from none other than Fujikura. He is the same old Fujikura, tough as ever. I'll write him back sometime. But he reproved me for having said, when I wrote you a while ago, "Let your *Manyoshu* pay tribute to me, in place of a sprig from the sacred tree," and at the moment I just can't explain my aspirations. Looks like you guys have a lot of lofty metaphysical conversations. Do you really have so much downtime in the Air Corps?

"Since the beginning of autumn, the sea grows rougher by the day where I am. I live in the waves and whistling winds, doused by the spray as I glide over the water. I study late into the night, with nautical almanac, tide tables, and pilots at hand. I don't have time to compose a poem or *tanka*. I am alone here. But you three *Manyo* scholars are still together, and you get along well. Don't alienate Fujikura. What he says is mostly true. And yet, granting all that . . . well, be that as it may, I just think we must set about preparing for our journey to the other world. That's the fate we shoulder."

I went to see Fujikura after dinner and asked, "What did you write to Kashima?" He didn't answer.

Kashima's postcard bore a red seal: "No Visitors." Evidently the torpedo boat crews endure a regime even stricter than ours.

We were granted liberty today in exchange for tomorrow's Sunday liberty, as a long spell of rain has rendered the airfield unusable. But nothing went my way today, and it was a very unpleasant excursion.

First, on the train to Beppu, Sakai started to crow, with exaggerated confidentiality, about what he claims is the real cause of Petty Officer D.'s suicide back at Izumi Naval Air Station. According to Sakai, the officer had VD. In a nosedive, the rapid acceleration dizzies even a healthy person, but if you are taking sulfa drugs, such as for the treatment of VD, aerobatics training is excruciatingly painful physically. And as a nosedive can leave you giddy for quite a while, it is unbearable mentally, too. The story itself wasn't much of a revelation. And while on the one hand I thought it could explain the incident, I wasn't really in the mood to hear that kind of story. Besides, Sakai unfolded his tale with ostentatious confidentiality, saying that he had heard it from the chief surgeon, and that we had better watch out for ourselves. He made such a fuss out of it that I was turned off by his tone. So, saying that I preferred to roam around by myself today, I parted with Sakai at Beppu Station. I also took leave of Fujikura, after we had all arranged to meet at Kajiya Inn in the evening.

I walked along Nagare-gawa Street toward the mountain. An aircraft carrier stood offshore, at anchor, and as I headed back I noticed a sign, "Navy Hour in Progress," hanging from the door of Senbiki-ya, a restaurant we had come by before. I dropped in, ate a persimmon and a fig, and was about to start in on a lunch of fried fish and pork cooked in soy sauce, when a lieutenant who was drinking at the next table addressed me. When I told him I was a student reserve officer at Usa Naval Air Station, he said, as if he wanted to pick a fight, "So what's your morale like? You must be depressed, having been dragged into this hopeless navy. Aren't you? Well, it's written all over your face."

"No, sir," I replied. "Everybody is in high spirits, especially after hearing the splendid results of the aerial engagement over Formosa. We are all itching to capitalize on the victory. We want nothing more than to master our skills as quickly as we can. And then we will set out to have our own duel with an enemy aircraft carrier."

The lieutenant soured and banged his beer glass on the table.

"Stop it with your big talk," he growled, glaring at me. I just gazed at his face for some time, startled. "Do you really believe the report that Imperial Headquarters issued?"

"Is it a problem if I do?" I answered back. Again, he burst out with a guffaw. Evidently he is assigned to the *Hosho*, the carrier anchored offshore. His uniform was soiled and a trench knife dangled over it. He was obviously quite drunk, and also, it appeared, thoroughly desperate.

"Do you want to know the truth?" the lieutenant said, and proceeded to inform me that a vast enemy task force had been steaming into Leyte Gulf since yesterday, accompanied by a number of attack transports that obviously intended to land.

"Do you think that America could endlessly bring out these aircraft carriers," he continued, "if we had been sinking them one after another? Do you think they are performing some kind of magic trick to produce these carriers?" Then he asserted that reports of the fighting at Formosa were riddled with cases where targets struck in night raids had been misidentified, and that the reports were also marred by wishful thinking.

"The war situation is fifty times worse than you think. The central command should reflect on what it is doing. The Navy Press Bureau ought to be straightened out. And *you*. Don't you talk so big, when you can't even fly like an honest-to-god pilot." He gulped down his beer, in terrible humor, and then he added, "Shall I dig potatoes? Do you want to see a crewman from a rattletrap carrier dig potatoes?" ("Dig potatoes" is navy slang for "tear this place apart.")

I wolfed down my lunch and excused myself, but I felt melancholy. It was astonishing that the Naval Academy could have produced, as I can only assume it did, an officer like this, but is there really any truth in what he told me? If, as this lieutenant maintains, we have been diving at oil tankers and landing craft and mistaking them all for aircraft carriers, then there is no reason why the enemy task force should be weakening. According to the lieutenant, the central command, half knowing what it was about, published its figures as an "official" report from Imperial Headquarters. But surely we men haven't all been mustered simply to embellish the front pages of newspapers with false numbers.

I had been wandering around in agitation, when it occurred to me that I intended to get a haircut, so I dropped into a barbershop along the seafront. A barbershop has a nice folksy smell about it. Tonic, cosmetics, steamed towels, and ear cleaning. I was somewhat able to calm myself at last, as I listened to the soothing sounds of the scissors.

I felt better by the time I left the barber's, so I decided to peek into a small shop of boxwood crafts. This area is noted for its boxwood.

> So busy!—the women divers of Shika,
> Cutting seaweed, roasting salt:
> They cannot spare a minute
> Even to take up a comb from the comb box.

> No thought now of taking up
> The boxwood comb from my comb box.
> Why should I adorn myself
> When you are not here to see me?

I remembered poems from the *Manyoshu* for the first time in quite a while, and I thought I would like to buy a fine, pretty boxwood comb for someone (actually, I had a concrete "someone" in mind from the outset). I debated a good long time before deciding on an elegant, rounded comb, which I arranged to have sent to Miss Fukiko Fukai in Minamata. An hour or so later I joined Fujikura and Sakai at the inn in Kamegawa Hot Springs that we treated rather like a boarding house. The two of them were already drinking orange wine and eating brown chicken sashimi. By that time I had started to regret having done such a thing behind their backs, and I fell into a deep gloom. It would have been different had the three of us sent the gift together. How will Fukiko and her parents take my having done so all on my own account? I rather doubt they will accept it without a second thought. I just wanted to express my gratitude and special affection. It will pain me if they ignore the gesture, and it will present another kind of problem if they accept it. I can't help feeling tenderness toward Fukiko. That's one thing. But it is another thing altogether for a man who will most likely die within a year to give voice to that sentiment. This can only disturb her, and also me, and to no good purpose. I decided to cancel the delivery, and tried, without success, to find the comb shop's telephone number.

What a foolish thing to do! A dull sense of melancholy always sets in after a day of liberty, and the incidents of today make me feel it all the more. I took a bath at Kajiya, emptied the bottle of orange wine, and, having said almost nothing, returned to base before ten.

OCTOBER 25

An alert was issued this morning: B-29s were flying over Cheju in four squadrons, making their way toward Japan. We sprinted out to field headquarters, and shortly thereafter ducked into the air-raid shelter.

Today's cloud index was nine. The ceiling was six to seven thousand meters, and the enemy aircraft flew at an altitude of about five thousand meters. As I took a peek out of the shelter, beautiful vapor trails emerged through the rifts in the clouds to the northwest, lengthening as the planes moved eastward. For the first time I heard the roar of American aircraft. I felt carefree, as if I were watching a sporting event.

These days we are constantly forced to forego training flights and my body is rusting away. Fuel supplies are very tight, and our allocation has been cut in half. We consider ourselves lucky if we get to fly every other day. Our training period has been extended accordingly, and now we are to receive our commission on December 25, three months behind schedule. The German army has withdrawn from Aachen. The Allies will penetrate the Rhineland. The defeat of Germany is in sight. What will ever become of Japan?

I happened to be next to the division officer in the shelter, so I asked him candidly about what I heard the other day from that lieutenant attached to the *Hosho*.

"Misidentification of targets isn't that unusual during a nighttime attack," he said, "but the reports issued by Imperial Headquarters are generally considered reliable. Even the enemy trusts them. I wouldn't expect to find any really significant or factitious errors. Truth be told, the *Hosho* can't withstand actual combat. She just hangs around the Seto Inland Sea for use as a training carrier. With her, it's the same as it is on warships like the *Yamashiro*. She tends to collect crewmen who fall behind in promotion, due to health problems or some such thing, and I wouldn't be surprised if they gripe whenever they get the opportunity out of smoldering frustration." I was a little relieved. I certainly have my gripes against the navy. But still, I have more faith in it than that lieutenant.

OCTOBER 29

Flights were canceled again.

News of a decisive sea battle in the Philippines. More magnificent results.

The commander-in-chief of the combined fleet had issued an urgent message: "Trust in divine favor and launch an all-out attack." And with that began a colossal naval engagement, in which the fleet employed its primary guns, an unusual thing these days. They say, however, that the enemy aircraft carriers swarming around Leyte Gulf number close to a hundred. This means that, even if we did in fact sink nineteen enemy carriers, it would hardly be a devastating blow. The material resources of the enemy astonish me.

"It's like fighting with King Kong," G. commented. We all laughed, though tensely.

When I heard that the warship *Musashi* was cruising along at twenty knots after absorbing six torpedoes, I took heart, thinking that the ship had lived up to its unsinkable reputation. But soon enough came news, strictly confidential, of its sinking. I'm at a loss for words. The greatest warship in the world is gone, the battleship over which I flew while at Izumi (the stunt that landed me in such hot water). I can only hope, desperately, that we are misinformed.

NOVEMBER 1

We were supposed to fly this afternoon, but the ring of a telephone put an end to that. A student in my outfit laughed in despair, bending backward in his chair.

I received a thank-you letter from Fukiko in which she said she really liked the boxwood comb. I hid the letter immediately, embarrassed by my act and conscious of others' eyes, though, needless to say, I opened it again when I went to bed at night, and read it over and over, three or four times. Apart from what she said in appreciation of the comb, the letter was simple and light, which was both a relief and a disappointment.

Afterwards I indulged myself in a daydream for quite some time, concerning which I am too embarrassed to write.

"Please send my best regards to Mr. Fujikura and Mr. Sakai," she said, but how can I send her best regards to them?

We did some repair work on the airfield this afternoon, draining it and filling it in with earth. In other words, it was hard labor. They are building a new runway on the eastern part of the field, in preparation for the 3rd Air Fleet's advance to Usa. Our task is to carry the surplus soil in rope baskets all the way back out here and fill in the hollows with it. The airfield is built over clayey soil and drains poorly. Consequently, it lacks the proper grading and is pocked with bumps. At 1630, the time set to stop, we had not yet completed half the task. A number of Korean laborers were assigned to the eastern runway, though only a handful were in fact applying themselves to the work, and the rest, several hundred in number, had no drive at all. They dawdled along for a spell, and then simply stopped altogether, staring about, vacantly. I gained a new idea of the Korean people, quite different from the sympathetic attitude I took when I was thinking about them in the abstract.

Speaking of airfield maintenance, I remember a story that an instructor told us. He said that enemy troops always seemed to land, whether on Guadalcanal, Attu, or elsewhere, just a scant week or so prior to the completion of construction work on our airfields. Our Corps of Engineers works unremittingly, and at great length, to build these airfields with manual labor, only to have them seized just before they are ready to be put in service. The enemy occupies them, easily finishes off the work with heavy equipment, and within a day or two begins using the fields to stage attacks against us.

During the Battle of Leyte Gulf, the 1st Air Fleet deployed an extraordinary unit called the Shinpu Special Attack Force (a.k.a., the "Kamikaze"). It seems the fighters were fitted out with special bombs, and the crews hurled themselves, planes and all, into enemy targets. Well, I suppose we won't get anywhere in this war unless we resort to drastic measures like that. Any man who wants to drop out, let him do it now. For my part, I no longer have any reservations about this kind of tactic. My only worry now is that I can't get up in the air. Who knows when I will fly the Type-97 solo.

They say the commander of the special attack force, a Lieutenant S., got his training in the carrier-based bomber unit here, and that he left Usa shortly before we arrived. The women at Senbiki-ya in Beppu wept at the news of the kamikaze attacks, remembering what the lieutenant had told them only a few days earlier: "If I die, lay out an offering of *shiruko* and fruit." So I'm told anyway.

NOVEMBER 5

Finally, after a long hiatus, we resumed training, starting with formation flights. From 500 meters up, I saw clearly just how bad this airfield is. Basically, it is nothing but a stretch of swamp. "Why don't we let the Yanks occupy the field for a while?" someone joked.

Flying in formation is hazardous. These aircraft don't shed their momentum as quickly as the intermediate trainers, and it's hard get a sense of space. I took three blows to the jaw for landing at seventy-five knots. I was fined one yen and fifty sen as well. M. had to cough up ten fifty-sen silver coins for damaging the tail of his plane as he taxied onto the apron.

Failing to erase the blackboard neatly costs you two fifty-sen pieces. They will rack up a considerable sum of money by the time we graduate, so long as we continue to fly. From the previous class they collected two thousand yen.

When we land, we tend to the aircraft. The undersides of the wings and fuselages are liable to be caked with dirt, especially if you glide in over the mud. It's quite a chore to wipe it all off.

Sunshine soon fanned out through the clouds, revealing a clear autumn sky. Young trainee pilots engaged in dive-bombing drills. Now and again they plunged, with an almighty roar, down over the field headquarters, almost to the point of crashing into it. Their planes dropped headlong, generating clouds at the wingtips. One came in especially low, scattering willy-nilly a flock of birds perched on the roof. If the pilot had pulled out just half a second later, he would have been a goner. When you're up in the air, you tend to be so preoccupied with precision, lest you get a dressing down, that the danger tends to escape your mind.

"Reading the personal remarks you submit," the chief flight officer commented, "I often come across such phrases as 'I must cultivate my character.' Indeed, it is important to cultivate your character. But what we want now are men who can win the war. We will welcome any miscreant at all, so long as he can hurt the enemy. Do the very best you can to cultivate *your skills.*" He makes perfect sense, of course, but it's not so easy to cultivate our skills when flights are canceled, day after day.

Flight rations were distributed again, all manner of new goodies, like wine, black tea, "energy food," an instant cinnamon drink.

As the sumo match set for the 14th approaches, the conflict between the recon students from the Naval Academy and us student reserves has been bursting to the surface. In any naval unit there is always considerable friction between Academy graduates and student reserves. On this particular occasion, however, we have a remarkably powerful lineup, including former collegiate sumo wrestlers, and the recon students have little chance of winning. The situation so frustrates them that they seize every possible occasion to pick at us, and deliver their corrections in the most spiteful of ways.

"Student reserves shall remain after everyone is dismissed," declared a recon student (a deck officer probationer, to be specific) at morning assembly today. Unfortunately, someone had left a book on military intelligence, strictly confidential material, on a desk during the special gymnastics course yesterday, and the recon students confiscated it. First, we endured a round of blows. These men aren't experienced at the business, but they certainly throw themselves into it, pounding away heavily. It is awfully painful.

"There is a reason why you are so careless with confidential material," said this deck officer probationer. "Namely, your spirit is more degraded than that of a common conscript, and you will receive a correction commensurate with that fact." He then proceeded to place conscripts' caps on each of us (they'd gathered them up from the barracks), ordering us all to "hold a push-up" for twenty straight minutes. It was mortifying. The eyes of some among us brimmed with tears. These Academy men are happy precisely insofar as they manage to bully us in the most humiliating way they can devise. It has nothing whatsoever to do with maintaining military discipline, or with "guiding" their junior comrades. Only six or seven of the ensigns among the recon students ever initiate this sort of conduct, with ten or so more chiming in. Many others adopt a courteous attitude toward us, but it is always the ruder fellows who take the lead on occasions like this. And we can't defy them head-on because a wall of rank stands between us.

When the second half of the 13th Class (our immediate predecessors) arrived at this base with their commissions, the recon students were still uncommissioned midshipmen. The reserve students actually outranked them. Even so, there was endless trouble, or so I hear. One day a recon student failed to salute a student reserve officer who happened to be an ensign, and the ensign struck him. That night the entire 13th Class was summoned to the lecture hall. "Student reserve officers are strictly subsidiary to men from the Naval Academy," they were informed. "It is absolutely outrageous for a student reserve to strike a graduate of the Naval Academy. You have sullied our illustrious tradition." At that absurd declaration, a bunch of lieutenants and lieutenants junior grade (instructors assigned to the recon students) ganged up to pommel the 13th Class. No doubt pent-up anger toward our predecessors is making the situation all the more difficult for us.

Let yourself be seen folding your arms, or whistling, or simply placing your hands in your pockets—not to mention inadvertently failing to salute—and a recon student will descend on you. However, he will not administer his correction on the spot. "Come see me at eight tonight," he will say, or "Come by after the special course," leaving you to spend hours in fear. And when you finally report to his quarters, he and his fellows all fall in just for the fun of a good thrashing. Sometimes they beat you right in the middle of the airfield so all the enlisted men can see. But for the moment we student reserves hold back our emotions, finding consolation in a sort of motto: "Exercise caution each day, and get satisfaction in the sumo match." The wrestlers' countenances change when they set in to practice. They look touchingly heroic.

The guidelines for the sumo match were announced yesterday. Each side is to field two teams of seven wrestlers, who will compete in a tournament. However, the recon students have been observing our practice sessions, and obviously they have concluded that they won't fare well against us. This afternoon they made a proposal: "Let's make it nine wrestlers each." When we declined, they came back with yet another proposal: "Then let's make it a round robin of fifteen wrestlers from each side." We asked why, but their reasoning was obscure. They are brewing something up, some way to pull rank on us so as to change the guidelines to their advantage. We once competed intercollegiately, in the catch-as-catch-can world of university students, but never once did we resort to such dirty tricks as these, no matter how desperately we wanted to win.

The recon students are all aged nineteen or twenty. They smoke and drink, some are already whoring around, and yet they are regarded by the public as the noblest of our warriors, as the very salt of the earth. The student reserves, "undermined by liberal education," are nothing more than an annoying, impure, and perfectly tiresome lot in the eyes of these recon students. How distorted and peculiar their pride is!

My mother has a younger brother in Kobe and years ago his second son Sadayuki got it into his head to attend a military prep school. His parents opposed the idea, but he persevered. The boy wasn't at home when my mother and I visited the family to congratulate them on his graduation, and I remember my uncle saying, with a wry grin, "Don't know, but it seems we've got something of a freak on our hands."

Only four days remain until the match. It appears that our instructors, Lieutenants Junior Grade S. and N. (both from the Naval Academy), are harboring mixed feelings.

NOVEMBER 13

Fujikura landed us in hot water again. Fine, let him stick to that defeatist attitude of his. The problem is that sometimes he goes too far. So long as he thinks and talks seriously, we give him an honest hearing, even when we disagree with him. But what he did today is inexcusable, as it entailed a good deal of trouble for others.

Seated beside the cigarette tray after lunch, Sakai was reading from the *Hagakure* when Fujikura stuck his nose into it. Written on the page were the four pledges of the samurai:

1. Thou shalt not fall behind in the Way of the Warrior
2. Thou shalt be of good service to thy lord
3. Thou shalt practice filial piety
4. Thou shalt be merciful and benevolent

Fujikura turned it all into a joke, rewording each entry:

1. Thou shalt not fall behind in the Realm of Famished Ghosts (a riff on the Buddhist Hell)

2. Thou shalt be of good service to thyself
3. Thou must understand that getting yourself killed is no way to practice filial piety

A recon student, Ensign Y., happened to be nearby making arrangements for tomorrow's sumo match, and he overheard Fujikura. Bloodthirsty as the atmosphere was, the recon students called him in at once. Fujikura returned some thirty minutes later, his face swollen up like a rock. The matter seems to have been referred first to the division officer, and then to the executive officer. Word soon spread that the blows might not fall on Fujikura alone, that the rest of us might be in for a correction, too, or else that Fujikura would take the blows and the rest of us be confined to barracks. Some reproached Fujikura, and others comforted him, but we were all apprehensive. However, toward evening, and rather more easily than we had expected, the affair was brought to a resolution. Only Fujikura and one other senior student were brought up before the executive officer.

"You've all got big mouths," the XO told Fujikura. "An officer has to learn how to rein in his tongue. And by the way, never confuse the *Hagakure* with 'Imperial Instructions to the Military.' The two things have nothing in common. There will be no need to pursue the matter any further. The recon students exceeded their authority. They overreached themselves, and I intend to admonish them. So don't worry, just put it out of your mind." That was an uncommonly fair decision. It turns out that the XO plays a pretty nice game. One fellow advanced a theory that he is a descendant of the masterless samurai who was expelled, during the so-called "cat-monster disturbance," from the Nabeshima clan and was later to produce the *Hagakure*.

Mr. Wang Ching-wei* has died in a hospital in Nagoya.

The day of the sumo match.

Purple curtains stretched around two sumo rings out behind the drill hall, and navy blankets, emblazoned with anchors, covered the four pillars. Facing the rings, seats were set up for the commander, the wardroom officers, and the officers of the first and the second gun rooms. To the left and right of these were seats for the recon students and the student reserves. Petty officers and enlisted men filled the seats further down.

The match was conducted as a tournament, according to the initial plans. From 1300 hours, the seamen divisions had their match. Once they had completed their semi-final bout, it was our turn to hold preliminaries. The bustle that had surrounded the rings gave way at once to complete silence, suffused with a kind of mute truculence. To a man, the wrestlers' adopted a fair-and-square attitude. Team 1 on our side won its match by a single point, but Team 2 lost, also by a point. This meant that Team 1 of the student reserves would compete with the recon students' Team 2 in the finals. Before that, however, the seamen had their final match, and the victory went to the carrier-based bomber trainees. But we took hardly any interest in anyone else's competition.

---

*Wang Ching-wei (1883–1944), rival of Chiang Kai-shek, was head of the government established in Nanking to administer Japanese-occupied China; he lived in Japan during the war and died in Nagoya.

Finally, our spearhead wrestler, Cadet Murase, faced off against Ensign K. The instant they rose from their crouches, they threw themselves into it, heaving against one another fiercely. Presently they moved into belt grips. First, Murase was pushed outward, his body arching back. My heart pounded, and I broke out in a cold sweat. I thought he was done for. But not for nothing had Murase earned his reputation in sumo back at Waseda University. With a wrapping maneuver, he freed himself, and, in a flash, he pushed his opponent out of the ring. A loud cheer went up. Our second wrestler brought us another win. We lost the third and the fourth bouts, won the fifth, and then lost the sixth. In the end, the contest came down to a match between the two team captains. Never have I witnessed a more exciting fight. Deafening cheers rang out from both sides. Our captain was Shirozaki, a Ritsumei-kan graduate weighing in at seventy-three kilograms. We had firm faith in him, but nonetheless our faces flushed, and all of us, without being aware of it, leaned forward in anticipation. Shirozaki himself, however, approached the ring with an air of perfect composure, stood up, and, without a hint of shakiness, easily dispatched his opponent with an overarm throw. For a moment we were struck dumb, but then came the applause. At last we had won, and our fortnight-long grudge was satisfied. It was a load off my mind. I felt as if I myself had been in the ring.

We returned to the barracks in triumph, in the excitement rapping each other on the shoulders for no good reason at all. "Hey, buddy!" "Hey yourself!" We talked of nothing but the sumo match. At dinner, our instructor, Lt.jg S., stopped by to eat with us. I was curious as to how he would behave, but he seems to be genuinely happy for us in our victory. In due course, our prize was brought in: a case of beer and two bottles of sake. A couple of ensigns from the 13th Class came over to thank the wrestlers. Also present were Lt. O. of the Aviation Maintenance Branch, Surgeon Lt.jg A., and Paymaster Lt.jg J. Next, yet another ensign from the 13th Class, a carrier-based bomber pilot who was good and soused, staggered over to congratulate us. They all looked immensely pleased. Clearly, the Naval Engineering College graduates, the surgeons and the paymasters—not to mention the students of the 13th Class—really had it in for the Naval Academy men. Practically everybody came by, except for the junior officers of the first gun room, all of whom graduated from the Academy.

We had agreed among ourselves to drink no more than half a bottle of beer each, but our visitors wouldn't leave it at that. Again and again they cried out, "Cheers!" "Bring more sake!" Aviation Maintenance Lt. O. reeled away, singing "Bring me sake, my true love," and back he came with a half-gallon jug. Paymaster Lt.jg J. sent his dog robber out to fetch his own personal ration of a dozen beers. And so the whole company went off on a mad drinking spree, singing military songs and overturning the dishes on the tables.

"Is our real enemy America or the Naval Academy?" someone asked. "We dedicate ourselves to Japan, but we don't intend to die for the Imperial Navy," declared someone else. At which a drunken Fujikura yelled out, "I don't intend to die for anybody!" I kicked him in the shin. Fortunately, in all the chaos his voice didn't carry.

The party finally ended when the command to "Prepare for the rounds" was issued. By that time, we had emptied one hundred eighty bottles of beer, seven half-gallon jugs of sake, and a considerable quantity of alcoholic beverages of a dubious nature. Each of us downed eleven apples and four oranges. Hard to believe how much we consumed. After the rounds I stood duty, my head spinning.

NOVEMBER 19

We had a spell of Indian summer days, with on-again/off-again training flights. But today at 2140, for the first time in a long while, Lt.jg S. ordered us all out on deck. We drew up, wondering what could be the matter. There seemed to be no call for a reprimand, now that the frenzy over the sumo match had subsided. The lieutenant showed up on the dot with a strained look on his face. He stared at us for some time.

"As of tomorrow, your training flights will cease." This was unexpected. "And there is no prospect of resuming them in the foreseeable future. No fuel is available. Japan staked the fate of the nation on Operation SHO-1 in the Philippines, and the results are anything but welcome." His emotions overcame him as he spoke, but he pressed on as if talking to himself, choking up from time to time. "We spoke of life and death, we talked about breaking through, but now we have nothing. Nothing at all is left us."

My mind went blank. I couldn't take it all in. In the month and a half since we arrived at Usa, we have had twelve days of flight training—in all, a mere ten hours and a smattering of minutes in the air. Now it looks as if the final battles may go on without us, that they may be lost to us forever.

As he wound things up, the lieutenant gave us a kind of placebo. "Surely you will be able to fly again, just as soon as we find a solution to the fuel problem. So don't let it get you down." As I climbed into my hammock, a flood of tears streamed down my face. I have finally shaken off my attachments to the things I once loved—to the campus, to the beauty of Kyoto and Yamato, and also to the *Manyoshu*. I have at last directed my mind into a single channel, and now they are telling me yet again to abandon what has become my sole purpose in life. We are absolutely forbidden to live freely. Will we now be denied the chance to die gracefully?

NOVEMBER 22

Sunday schedule. Liberty.

My father phoned unexpectedly last night, saying that he was in Beppu and wanted to see me. I went directly to the Hinago Inn, diverting myself along the way with speculations as to the occasion for the visit, but what I heard on entering the room was that my brother Bunkichi is dead.

My dad says he presumably died with honor, together with his outfit on Tinian Island, toward the end of September. I had feared something like this would happen. My father couldn't bring himself to break the news in a letter, and what with the unbearable loneliness, he decided to arrange the family business so as to find time to see me personally. My mother had totally broken down when she heard. I thought about how she will feel when I'm killed, too.

Placed on one of the staggered shelves in the room was my brother's photograph, as a senior private in the Japanese Army. He looked melancholy. There was a glassiness about his eyes, and his uniform was a bit too big. He differed from me in personality, educational background, and circumstances. Above all, he wasn't young anymore. I imagine he lacked the youthful momentum that allows me and my comrades to coast along in military life. To him, everything must have been downright torture. In what way could his death possibly have helped arrest the decline of the Japanese forces? He must have died in perfect sadness, seeing himself as a weak soldier, and probably of little use for anything. I wish we could have let him live quietly, tucked away in some home unit in inland Japan.

I bathed alone. Unlike the inn at Kamegawa, this one is equipped with a fine bath. Pure, sweet water springs up abundantly from below. I can't believe that people who depart this world dwell in some kind of a "heaven," with bodies like our own. But I have no difficulty imagining that they are, body and soul, resolved into the natural universe, that they are translated back into water, into mist, into the leaves of the mountain trees. Two months have passed. My brother must already have returned to the tidal currents of the ocean, to the autumn clouds, and to the wells of this hot spring. I stirred the smooth waters for a long time.

When I came out of the bath, the meal was already laid out. My father had asked the maid to serve the sake he brought with him, a brand called "Sakura Masamune." There he sat, sipping sake and eating prawn tempura, in front of my brother's photograph. I changed into a padded kimono and took a seat opposite him. The people at the inn called me "young master," which made me feel a bit iffy. But our maid very much resembled Fukiko, in features and in carriage, and as I mellowed, I felt like dropping a few hints about Fukiko, in the way a schoolboy might. But I dissuaded myself. I would certainly have told my father about her if the war were over, and he might have taken pleasure in listening to the story.

He gave me an heirloom dagger, which had been made by Kenroku, a pupil of Seki-no Magoroku. There was a scratch on the blade, probably made by a whetter, but it had a superb metallic smell. After the meal, we walked toward the shore of Shonin-ga-hama. The wooden clogs felt pleasant on my bare feet. The mountains in Beppu were ablaze with autumn colors. White plumes of steam rose up from the springs among the trees with their elegant lines. The ocean was bright, blue and clear. Waves lapped gently at the rocks, and then ebbed. Along the shore, hot water bubbled up here and there and streamed into the sea, leaving yellowish tracks among the stones.

"Before you were born, I came to Beppu with your mother and brother," my father said. "And he sat down right there, along Nagare-gawa Street, and refused to budge an inch until I bought him a toy." He smiled sorrowfully.

We returned to the inn around three o'clock, bathed again, and had dinner. My father returns home by boat tomorrow morning, so I took my leave and headed for the base.

The moon is five days old, so it was dark in the train. Still, Sakai, Fujikura, Murase, and a few others were all on board, and they consoled me for the loss of my brother.

NOVEMBER 25

Two carrier-based attack bombers, called the "Tenzan," were brought in by air transport. The men put them through their paces, gunning the motors full throttle. The propellers made a tremendous roar. Several mechanics clung to the tail of each plane to keep it grounded, but even so, the planes bore down hard on the chocks with their wheels, making creaking noises. I felt envious. A torpedo was clasped to the fuselage of each Tenzan with two cables. I always thought torpedoes were slung directly underneath the body, but these were fastened a little to the right of center to allow, as I understand it, for the propeller wash and the gunsights.

Now that flights have been suspended, we do formation training on bicycles. Military discipline, including our reports to field headquarters, is as strict as it ever was during regular flight training, but otherwise, we just ride around the apron on bicycles, with model aircraft in tow. In other words, any practice we get is utterly useless.

No report on the status of the war. We have no information as to how our forces in the Philippines are being supplied, nor any idea whether effective measures have been taken to cut off the enemy's lines. Nothing but ominous silence. I hear we can now count our regular aircraft carriers on the fingers of one hand, and that we can count our remaining cruisers on the fingers of two. The carriers *Zuikaku* and *Zuiho* are both gone. According to Lt.jg S., the enemy's raid on Omura the other day destroyed a number of the new "Ryusei" carrier-based attack bombers, together with all the other aircraft that had just come off the line at the Aeronautical Arsenal. The planes were awaiting assignment when two hundred of them were destroyed in eight successive strikes. I wonder why they didn't take to the air and flee. Furthermore, Omura Air Station is a fighter base, so why didn't the fighters scramble when they learned enemy planes were over Cheju? Also, I hear that one hundred fighters en route to the Philippines were picked off by a mere four enemy aircraft. Most were shot down. The excuse is that our fighters were unarmed at the time, as they were to be armed when they reached their destination. But their destination was a battlefield! It's totally ridiculous. Word came in, too, that we produced three new four-engine long-range heavy bombers called the "Renzan," and that two of them crashed during test flights. Some wag dubbed it "Self-Defeating Aerial Battle." I can't shake off the feeling that we are dancing to the enemy's tune.

Tonight we watched a movie titled *The Twenty Thousand Kilometer Front*, which was not much more than parts of old newsreels cobbled together. Watching these images, most of which date from around the time we captured Singapore, I was overcome by the conviction that we are living in a completely different era.

NOVEMBER 30

No flights.

Time passes drowsily. We eat, do "formation flights" on bicycles to ease our minds, eat yet again, read novels, and sleep, and that's about all we do. Recently, all maki-zushi has vanished from the canteen, leaving buns with azuki-bean paste standing alone on the shelf. However, rations of roasted seaweed are plentiful, so breakfast is quite good. Turnips show up every day as pickles. The pickles have a faint preservative odor, but I enjoy their radishy bite.

To possess a robust body, with a healthy appetite for food and sex; to employ the mind well and often; to bequeath to the next generation superior offspring and a real intellectual inheritance: *that* is the ideal life for a man. However, the national crisis compels us to curb certain aspects of our character, both physical and spiritual, and to develop certain other aspects to unnatural extremes. We have accepted the situation, and have done our best to accommodate ourselves to it. But now we find ourselves thrown into a life where we just stuff our bellies, engage in pointless physical labor, and then sleep it all off. I can't imagine a more miserable situation for any man who wishes to get a sense of what he really is. Some indulge themselves in pleasure, precisely as if they didn't want to "fall behind in the Realm of Famished Ghosts," using their status as navy warbirds for cover. These men I used secretly to regard as "fighting pigs," but now it seems we are all " *non*-fighting pigs."

Exams. An epidemic of fraud. And no wonder the epidemic spreads, because why on earth should "pigs" learn the theory of celestial navigation? I don't peek at others' exam papers myself, but I let my neighbors sneak a look at mine. And if I don't cheat, it's not because I hate the fraud, but because I don't give a damn about my grades.

I grow terribly forgetful. Not being able to recollect what I was thinking only the night before is getting to be an everyday affair. The English word for "kawa" slipped out of my memory, and I couldn't find it again for the life of me. I asked Sakai, but he said he didn't know, either.

"Wouldn't 'river' do?" said a fellow who'd overheard us, making a face.

"Yes, that's it. It's 'river.'" We laughed.

Still no flights.

A certain Lt.jg Tanaka came on deck toward evening to have a little talk with us. He is a stout man and holds a fifth rank in judo. He had been making a sortie to the Philippine Islands when bad visibility forced him to make a landing at Oita; that's how he ended up here. He described to us how the aircraft carrier *Ryu-jo* went down just east of Bougainville Island in August 1942. On board the sinking ship, he almost suffocated from the smoke and had to sustain himself on the air trapped in desk drawers. "Just look at you," his superior officer had said, "what are you sucking at when you're about to die anyway?" And yet, he managed to survive. Now he is attached to a special attack force of carrier-based "Suisei" bombers. He will head for the Philippines as soon as the weather clears. Once there, he will take to the air outfitted lightly, with neither a reconnaissance crew nor machine guns—in fact, carrying nothing but a No.80 (800 kg) bomb, lashed to the plane with straw rope. He will make his charge at 350 knots.

"I'll receive a special promotion," he said, "jumping two ranks at once. Soon I will be a lieutenant commander." He smiled. Obviously you can give up your life, but not your honor. Whatever the case, this lieutenant has only ten days or so left to live.

He had more news, too, about the so-called "human torpedoes," or "Kaiten," and also about the German V-1. The V-1 is said to be smaller than a Link trainer, with wings less than two meters long. The Germans bomb the city of London with it, using radio-control. We don't have the technology to control a plane by radio. So instead we place a man into a small, rocket-propelled craft similar to the V-1. It flies at 600 kilometers per hour for two minutes, with a range of thirty-five miles. After that the thing just glides until it crashes into the target. A Type-1 or Type-96 land-based attack bomber hugs this flying bomb to its belly until the target is within range. The device is so small that, once the pilot is on board, it can carry only one No.25 (250 kg) bomb at most. Consequently, even if it hits the target directly, it does little damage. It seems the "human torpedo" is a little more effective.

I can honestly say that I need no double promotion, and that I have no wish to be a war hero, but I have to wonder: Am I really content to crash headlong into an enemy ship knowing all the while that my sacrifice cannot possibly destroy it?

DECEMBER 9

A fourth December 8th has come and gone, with no good results to show for it. The "divine winds," the "kamikaze," seem to be blowing in the wrong direction. Anyway, today the wind comes in strong from the west, and I can see, through the windowpanes of the ordnance classroom, the occasional flurry of snow. It's pretty cold for Kyushu at the beginning of December.

An inquiry from the OD's room arrived this afternoon. "We're putting on a show. Do any of you student reserves want to join in?" We agreed to do it. After all, we still want to feel the breeze of the free world.

"Look. Some broad is headed for the drill hall," a fellow said.

"She's wearing silk stockings," said another.

For all the fuss we made, the show turned out to be a bore. The singing and dancing were low camp, teasing our sexual desire to no good purpose, grimly rekindling old dormant dreams. And then came a speech from the city hall clerk in charge of the event. "We devote ourselves to our modest art. Blah-blah-blah." It disgusted me. What we need is fuel, or, failing that, to be allowed to return to campus as free men. Nothing else will console us. I haven't heard anything from Kyoto lately.

They say, "Nothing can wait in the air." Failure always means the end. Airmen are meant to live life to the absolute fullest, every single day, but our lives at this base are empty and dull, every single day. What should I do?

DECEMBER 14

"Battle stations! Battle stations!" The warning came in yesterday around half past one. A large formation of enemy bombers was moving north over Chichi-jima Island. And today the morning papers report that some eighty B-29s raided Tokyo, Shizuoka, and Aichi. It looks like Saipan and Tinian are rapidly taking shape as major enemy bases for strategic bombing. My brother's body must be cast off somewhere in the corner of an airfield, his bones laid bare to the rains. According to the papers, damage from the B-29s wasn't severe, but I worry that the raids might have aggravated the damage already done by the earthquake that struck the Tokai district just the other day.

We had a visitor from Tokyo. He says they suffered successive raids on November 24, 25, 26, 29, and 30. Gotanda Station is completely destroyed. And the used-bookstore district around Kanda is a stretch of wasteland.

"Does that mean such-and-such place now has an unobstructed view of X?"

"So that store is gone now, too, huh?"

Whinnying like horses, the Tokyo men in our outfit cajoled one another.

"It's no laughing matter," they conceded, amid guffaws, "but what else can you do?"

A mood of defeat pervades the metropolis, our visitor says, and conditions at the aircraft factories, etc., are not so rosy as the newspapers and the radio would have us believe. Recently, the workers have been staging ever more serious slowdowns. I cannot approve of such behavior, but I can imagine how easily these men fall apart, once they've been stripped of hope and pride. Even at this air station we had an incident. An unidentified man called headquarters repeatedly, until he was good and satisfied that the commander himself was on the line. Then he let the curses fly. "You blockheaded murderer! You should be the first to die!" It was determined that the call came from inside the base, but those in charge decided not to pursue the matter. Well, it's okay by me if they don't, but the constant internal squabbling, the rumors, the general collapse of discipline—it is all the sign of a nation in decline. For my part, I will attend more closely to military discipline, and if at times I have to correct the enlisted men, so be it.

According to the newspaper, the U.S. Navy has now developed a prototype for a new fighter plane whose payload exceeds that of our dive-bombers, and whose top airspeed is 1,020 kilometers per hour, which is just shy of the speed of sound (1,200 kph). It translates into 680 knots, or twice the speed of our standard 300 knots. The Americans have produced a real menace. They say the enemy lost eighty-eight aircraft carriers during the past year, but I don't know if I can blindly trust that figure. All I know for sure is that we have only three or four carriers left on our side.

Training flights are supposed to resume in mid-January, but for the time being we are completely shut out of the sky. Everything is in a slump. We enjoy an abundance of oranges (as a matter of fact, we each received ten today), but that's only because this region produces a lot of oranges and they can't ship them out due to reductions in carrying capacity.

Today's lecture was on radio homing, direction-finding, and the protocols for carrier-based takeoff and landing. I'm no good at theory, and when I don't follow the lecture, I get sleepy, and when I fall asleep, I get a chill. Anyway, what's the use of learning how to take off and land on carriers that we no longer possess? Forty-five men from the Army Air Corps are bunking at the drill hall these days to attend the navy lectures. They even hauled in a huge navigation drawing board for the purpose. I guess the Army finally sees the need to master modern scientific methods of navigation. But I have to say, they are, as always, a few steps behind, and it is getting late in the day.

DECEMBER 18

Cadet S.'s father died of a rare disease in which blood clots block up the capillaries. He traveled to Tokyo to attend the funeral and returned to base last night.

According to the information S. brought back, the damage Tokyo suffered in the raids isn't quite as bad as we imagined. The fire brigades did a tremendous job, managing to contain most of the damage from the incendiary bombs. He could see the B-29s flying in at 8,000 meters, mere dots in the sky. And though he couldn't make out the fighters, he knew they were there because they gleamed as they rolled over. We fire our high-angle guns relentlessly, but the enemy bombers evade them. The student service units are really pitching in, devoting themselves body and soul. Apparently, it's the regular factory hands who generally lack discipline. As for the ordinary people: They still have the heart to browse around the Ginza, outfitted in gaiters, gas masks, and tin hats. They even staged a concert in Hibiya. Unmistakably there are fewer men around. On the other hand, the earthquake damage all along the Sea of Enshu is worse than we thought. The railroad bridge over the Oh-i River collapsed, totally disrupting transportation and distribution networks. Recovery along the Tokaido Line simply isn't a prospect this year. It was amusing to see how curious we were to hear S.'s report. We were all ears, as if he had been to Persia or Egypt.

On Saturday morning, somewhere out behind the lavatory and the barracks, someone struck a seaman for failing to salute, and at around 11 o'clock today the culprit was ordered to reveal himself. The seaman suffered a broken cheekbone, and according to the chief surgeon's examination, the injury might permanently impair his ability to chew. He claims a student reserve officer corrected him. Well, the incident has already surfaced, and unless the perpetrator comes forward, they say the case will be referred to a court martial. So, after lunch, every student reserve who punched a seaman on Saturday went to the sick bay to meet the boy, one by one. But he didn't finger any of us. I went, too, having corrected a petty officer for failing to salute me out by the swimming pool Saturday morning. I wasn't in any danger, since my set-to obviously involved a different man at a different place, but the whole event set me to brooding again. Just a few days back I resolved to strike enlisted men if I thought it would help maintain discipline, but in truth, the impulse to strike doesn't necessarily spring from high-minded deliberation. More often than not, "maintaining discipline" is just the excuse we use to blow off steam.

The seaman with the broken cheekbone will probably be sent back out into the free world. He certainly has my deepest sympathy. He returns to his parents a cripple, and not because of a battlefield injury, but because of a blow he took for failing to salute. What will the villagers say? What will his parents think of the navy? And how will he make a living for the rest of his life? I have decided not to raise my hand against anyone after all.

Fujikura saw me go off to sick bay, and when I got back, he said, "If you really think you can save Japan by dying, go ahead and die. I won't stop you. But even *you* don't really believe you can save the country by beating up a seaman, now, do you? If you engage in this sort of behavior to vent your indignation over blows you took from recon students or instructors, why don't you strike back at *them* instead? Think about the feelings of those seamen recruits, men who can't vent their anger on anybody. Maybe skipping the occasional salute is the only way they have to relieve their frustration. I don't care if they don't salute me. And if what you call 'military spirit' continues to manifest itself like this, well, I may really lose my patience with you."

I had already thought better of my earlier resolution when Fujikura let loose on me, and his words got on my nerves. "It's none of your business," I retorted, "who do you think you are anyway? You flatter yourself with your great humanity and civility, but you're nothing but an egotist." I continued in that vein for a spell. Lately, Fujikura has drifted away from the other men in our division. I have little contact with Sakai, as he is in the bomber division, and I miss Kashima immensely, probably because we are so far apart.

But as for that injured seaman, his story gradually changed as the day wore on, and the details are now obscure. The account differs according to whom he tells it to. Now it's not even certain that the perpetrator was a student reserve. Judging from all the information, he was likely punched either by an assistant division officer (a special services officer), or else by one of the veteran petty officers, the men seamen fear the most. But this seaman couldn't bring himself to name the offender, and when he was questioned he laid the blame on the student reserves, the men with whom he has the least contact anyway. It was all a first-rate nuisance for us student reserves, but I felt for his situation.

As night fell, the top brass sent down a message: "If all student reserves swear they have not harmed this seaman, we will accept your word and consider the case closed." They are adopting an air of great magnanimity. It's strange, though, that they should so easily settle a matter that might well have merited a court martial. It makes me suspicious. From the point of view of the men at the top, the perpetrator must be very inconveniently situated.

Last night there was a titanic storm. Gales gathered from the four corners of the universe to smash us, and I felt the rumbling in my gut. After that, a blizzard set in, and it has been snowing all day long. At first, the soft cottony flakes vanished when they touched the ground, precisely as if they had been sucked into it, but soon enough they started to pile up, and when the sun finally peeked out, the snow in front of the motor pool glittered. It really was lovely.

Flights are still suspended. The enemy has landed on Mindoro. Three oil tankers are said to have made port at Kure, under an imposing escort, but from the looks of it our fuel won't arrive for a while yet. Beginning on the 26th, the carrier-based bomber group will fly Type-99s. The prospect sends them into raptures, as they are to graduate to the Type-99 before they've even completed the regular course in the Type-96. The Type-99, it seems, can burn alcohol fuel without much retrofitting. There was talk of our resuming flights, too, once we obtain the fuel. But our Type-97 attack bombers can't tolerate alcohol fuel without a thorough refitting of both tank and carburetor, so the plan has been scratched.

Lieutenant Commander F. lectured this afternoon on the art of signal communication. Then he gave us a lesson in combat based on the Battle of Leyte Gulf, focusing particularly on the special attack force. Incidentally, he also described, in detail, the destruction of our airfield at Tainan (in Formosa). That field is now totally unusable, with the result that the Tainan Air Corps has been disbanded, its crews and aircraft dispersed to various bases. Many came to Usa, Lt. Cdr. F. among them.

His account of the decimation of Tainan is as follows.

Thirty or so Grumman fighters came in first, gaining command of the skies around the airfield, and here is how they did it: The enemy fighters approached in a stacked formation, the lower squadron flying in at 300 meters with a "rising sun" emblem painted on their wings (*that* was a base tactic). Some claim that the emblems actually changed, in accord with special beams of light emitted from their sister-planes: the rising sun one minute, U.S. insignia the next. But however that may be, our men were led to believe, all the way up to the bitter end, that these fighters had come to assist them. Our twenty Zeroes were shot down the second they took to the air. Next, Grumman carrier-based bombers flew in to attack. Their bombsights are very precise, and most of our hangars and other facilities were destroyed by direct hits on dive-bombing runs. I should say in passing that America's bombsights (could they be radar-assisted?) have recently attained a formidable degree of accuracy: a margin of thirty meters from an altitude of 8000 meters. Also, there are a number of female pilots among the U.S. Navy. One of them went down in a parachute, and a native Formosan chased her, wooden stick in hand. When she was captured, she purportedly insisted that somebody "Show me the guy who shot me down!"

An account on the special attack force followed.

At that time, the 1st Air Fleet, commanded by Vice Admirals Teraoka and Onishi, had a scant total of forty aircraft, damaged but viable. Our surface force managed to inflict some damage on the enemy, but they were soon slaughtered by a new relay of U.S. carriers, and the surviving vessels had precious little chance to make an escape. This was when the *Musashi* went down. Some two hundred fifty fighters came in from the 2nd Air Fleet. Of these, a little more than a dozen suffered damage without even fighting, owing to adverse conditions at the base. When the balance of the fighters launched their attack a swarm of Grummans descended on them, and half of our planes were shot down before ever reaching a target. And the story goes that, as a last resort, and hoping to recover from the assault, the 1st Air Fleet ordered out the Kamikaze force. Lieutenant S. had been down with diarrhea, but he folded up his bedding and went out to lead the attack. Many objected to the decision to use such a tactic, despite the fact that the lieutenant deeply wished to make the sortie. But as things stand now, this "human bullet" tactic has been systematically and permanently adopted by Imperial Headquarters. In point of fact, all the instructors at Tainan had already been organized into "special attack forces," even before the base was wiped out.

When I heard this, I said to myself, "I will die, too." Suddenly I felt the bottom drop out. It was as if something had been torn from inside my body. Ostensibly, I had long been prepared to die, had long been ready to become a "human bullet," or whatever. But even so, I was hollowed out, and I groaned aloud before I knew it. Then the next moment my attitude wheeled about, and I said to myself, "Damn it all to hell! Let's just knock them off!" It's odd. Obviously I had wanted to survive, and had been fooling myself all along, believing that I was really prepared to die. And now that my death is a near certainty, I feel as if I'm living in a dream.

Next year's call-up will be for six thousand new recon men and six thousand new pilots, a total of twelve thousand men. No doubt these rosy-faced youths will be organized into "special attack forces," just like the young warriors of Byakko-tai mustered to fight during the Boshin war. But how on earth will the navy come up with the aircraft and the fuel to make it all possible?

DECEMBER 25

We are commissioned. At nine o'clock we hoisted the navy flag and bowed in the direction of the Imperial Palace, with the "cherry blossom" pins of ensigns on our collars. Technically we were inducted last night, the moment we were officially relieved of the title "Student Reserve." As of today we begin our duty under instruction.

I don't feel particularly emotional. When graduates of the Naval Academy receive their commission they celebrate with a big bash, a whole forest of sake and beer, but no special event marks the occasion for us. We were supposed to be granted an outing immediately after the ceremony, but instead found ourselves placed on Defense Condition 2, as the report came in that an enemy plane was approaching Omura, and a whole formation was over Cheju. When the alert was called off at 1005, we were free to go. We stopped in at the Brotherhood of Enlisted Men to buy gaiters and a pair of slippers, which made me feel like a full-fledged *something* anyway. Then we headed for Beppu on the 1116 semi-express.

The weather was mild, which seemed a waste on a day of liberty. I ordered a simple lunch of yam-and-rice porridge at our usual spot, the Kajiya Inn in Kamegawa. With a huff and a puff, I slurped down the boiling hot bowl of thick, sweet soup. It was good.

I wrote to my father, to Professors O. and E., to Kashima, and also to several others, with news of our commission. I also wrote to Fukiko. This I did under the joint names of Sakai, Fujikura, and myself, although I felt a little twinge, like the prickle you get in your chest as you drink sparkling water.

At night, to celebrate, the proprietress at Kajiya served us a half-gallon of sake on the house. Thanks to her, we had plenty to drink with our blowfish stew. The octopus tempura was tasty, but the testis of the blowfish is an indescribable delicacy. We had a little debate as to whether you feel pain when you die from blowfish poisoning. Some people say yes, some say no. And from there the conversation shifted to a debate as to whether or not you suffer when crashing into an enemy ship on one of those "special attack" missions. I expect I will lose consciousness before sensing any pain, and anyway my body will be scattered to the winds on impact. So, all things considered, I voted for the "no-pain" theory. Sakai believes that he will suffer excruciating pain for the second or so it takes for his life to be extinguished. But this is doomed to be a barren controversy because nobody has ever returned from such a mission to tell the tale. Fujikura just listened in silence, his knees drawn up.

We met a pretty little girl on the train back. I gave her two "eyeballs"—vitamin-rich snacks used for high-altitude and duration flying. I always carry a few in my pocket. Her mother was so gratified that she offered me a parcel in return. I declined the gift, but Fujikura barged in with a "Thank you, ma'am" and snatched up the package. He was quite drunk, but he was a bastard nonetheless.

When we disembarked at Yanagiga-ura, we opened the package to find six rice cakes, and with azuki bean-paste no less. I felt much obliged to see two vitamin supplements metamorphosed into six *an-mochi*. The mother and the daughter were bound for Monji.

Incidentally, it seems children these days are brought up precocious, a whole pack of junior scientists and junior nationalists. Well, adults have to stop building an artificial world for their children. Kids should never be deprived of the chance to wallow in the mud and climb trees. They need their butterflies, their mountains and rivers. Let our generation die off, and let the coming generation enjoy a new and auspicious era, an era of real liberty and prosperity.

JANUARY 1, SHOWA 20 (1945)

Sunny. Reveille at four. Departed at 0430 in military uniform to worship at Usa Shrine. Returned at seven. Hoisted the naval ensign at eight, followed by a bow in the direction of the Imperial Palace. At 1000 all at the rank of warrant officer or above drank in celebration in the drill hall. No lunch together. Immediately went out for an excursion.

It was festive on the train, as might be expected. Women in their best kimonos, red-faced drunken peasants— everything contributed to the rustic New Year's atmosphere. But my mind was preoccupied with thoughts of my family and of the Fukais of Minamata. I wonder how they are faring. This year will probably see the end of my life. This New Year's holiday will be my last. On one of the three hundred sixty-five days of Showa 20 my obituary will be written. My brother Bunkichi is already dead, and when I consider how hollow my parents' lives will be after I, too, die, I regret that they didn't have more sons. I hope they will seriously consider adopting a child.

I had quite a few rice cakes today, as though I were trying to mark the New Year by eating them. However, in these parts *zoni* isn't very good, as they don't use any miso (the same goes for the Tokyo area). I crave the Kyoto-Osaka version of this traditional New Year's soup, with its rich base of white miso.

JANUARY 7, FEAST OF THE SEVEN HERBS OF HEALTH

I pulled second shift as probational assistant officer of the day, half past eleven to half past five. All manner of business flows in, but in spurts. I don't really understand any of it, so I just keep a straight face and say "Roger," no matter what comes my way, and then the clerks and the sentries handle it. The trainees are pouring back in from their holiday excursions, faces flushed by the cold winds, but still in the warm embrace of the family hearth.

"So-and-so of the Xth Division has just returned, sir."

"Roger that."

"Thank you for the time back home, sir."

"Roger." That's the way it works.

At about 1530, a Type 99 Carrier Bomber crashed. I thought we had yet another martyr, but the pilot came out all right. It was Ensign K., my 14th Class comrade. He was grinning. He knew he wouldn't be reprimanded, as he remembered well what Lt.jg E. said some time ago: "I've already wrecked six airplanes. Any man who's scared to bang up a plane or crack a fart is good for nothing. Don't let it get to you."

Ensigns Tsubota, Nakame, and Tsukamoto have left this air station. *Please meet with a death that shall be a model for us all,* I prayed.

A while ago, a Lt.jg Tanaka briefly sojourned here after making an emergency landing in Oita, and he told us all about the Kaiten and the German V-1 rocket. Word comes in now that he made his sortie to the Philippines as planned, perishing gracefully in a Suisei carrier bomber attached to the special attack force.

They keep a monkey named Hanako in the medical ward, and at around 1710 notice came in that a petty officer had made her eat three cigarettes. Of course, I was busy enough as it was, without having to file a report because a monkey ate three cigarettes. I went over and told that petty officer off. Hanako looked perfectly fine, though, behaving as if nothing had happened.

It was not until my watch ended and I had some dinner that I felt any relief.

My memory is really going these days. It's not just peoples' names or foreign words that I forget. I'm uncertain, for example, even about the total number of poems in the *Manyoshu.* All kinds of things just slip out of my head, and apparently the problem is chronic. I peeked into my diary to help myself remember what I did during the New Year's holiday last year, and found that we made our first excursion from Otake Naval Barracks, and also that I had grown a trifle sentimental gazing at the waters of the Iwakuni River. Yes, I remember now: We were wearing our sailor's caps. The memory materializes like an old, old dream.

I've read quite a few books since we stopped flying, but these, too, are swept from my mind, one after another. Partly this is because I just don't come across any really good books. Mostly I read novels, not poetry, but unless it is a truly great work, a novel will only do you harm.

U.S. troops finally landed at Lingayen Gulf. Pouring down a storm of shells and bombs, they climbed onshore with their tanks in the lead. According to reports, even our reconnaissance planes launched desperate attacks, but there is no word about the result. The enemy is said to have a tremendous number of Grumman fighters for cover. Our special attack forces can hardly even make it to their targets. This is especially true in the case of carrier-based attack bombers. If they make a sortie in the daytime, hugging their torpedoes, they are wiped out before they ever reach the enemy. As for the army's Hayabusa fighters, these are reputedly helpless against the B-29s. They are unable to approach them, let alone crash into them. Given this state of affairs, what difference would it make even if we had thousands of aircraft? Apparently, the war has progressed to the last stage in this cycle of our nation's rise and fall.

This morning a Type-96 carrier bomber crashed. Later, this afternoon, a Type-99 bomber touched down only to catch fire on the runway and promptly go up in smoke. Only the tail remained. This happened when we were about to commence the special course. As black smoke plumed up from the airfield, we dashed out. The loudspeakers sounded off: "First Rescue Unit, deploy!" and there was the Type-99, gliding along in flames. When we arrived, it was ablaze at the end of the apron, its duralumin alloy emitting intense white light, only the tail and engine still recognizable. Red flame in a fat column of black smoke, a blinding incandescent blaze at the core: transfixed by the sight, I thought that these will be the colors under which we depart this world. Mysterious, solemn colors. There must be something wrong with the alcohol fuel, as crash landings of carrier bombers are now a daily routine. Fuel and flight tests were completed today for the carrier attack bombers, too, and before long our training flights should finally resume. If we are to burn alcohol fuel, though, we must be extra careful. They say that when the temperature inside the cylinders drops to 150 degrees Celsius, the propellers will stop. The last thing I want to do is die in an accident, but inevitably some among us will.

A cat has been meowing for days now, somewhere in the barracks. Who knows, maybe it gave birth to a litter of kittens in the attic. But whatever the cause, it keeps meowing uncannily, day-in and day-out, gradually shifting its location. They tell us to catch the cat and zap it, but we don't know where it is. I can't help regarding it as an evil omen in light of the recent chain of accidents.

JANUARY 15

Yet another Type-99 crash-landed today. Also, when one of our Type-96 bombers pulled into the approach path and closed its throttle, the propellers seized and the plane almost crashed into the ground. Still, the two crewmen were OK. Everyone thought they were done for, but they emerged with only a few minor injuries to the head and face. And though they griped about the pain, their lives didn't seem to be in any danger. Day after day, we watch planes crash or flip over, with the 1st and

2nd Rescue Units deployed. Considering the frequency of accidents, though, there have been relatively few casualties, thanks entirely to the shoulder straps. If we suffer the same sort of accident in a carrier *attack* bomber, which is not equipped with shoulder straps, we will surely die on the spot, our skulls shattered. No matter what the cost, we simply must equip our Type-97 carrier attack bombers with shoulder straps before resuming flights. Reportedly, they are having a fair number of accidents of unknown cause at Hyakuri-hara Air Station, too, using alcohol fuel.

A recon student called before lights out and summoned us.

"Before today's lesson, one of you guys was wearing a shirt during calisthenics. Everyone assemble in the officers' lounge." Now, just the other day a senior officer said it was all right for us to wear shirts, so we went to the lounge and pleaded, explaining what the officer had told us. But it was all in vain. Some of us got the maximum of seven blows, some got the minimum of two, and I got five. Afterwards, we were made to run, double time, two circles around the apron, or about four kilometers. We were drenched in sweat on a cold winter night. We thought we would certainly be dismissed after that. Wrong. They hauled us out to the grounds (it had started to rain) and ordered us to do knee-bends combined with an exercise where we throw our arms up at an angle: four hundred fifty repetitions. We endured it well. Then, our backs and legs quaking, we crawled back to the barracks, hunched forward as if with an acute bellyache, and barely able to support our bodies. On my shaky legs, it's dangerous to walk down a staircase. I have to say this is a lunatic way of correcting us.

And how do the recon students perform at calisthenics? On cold, snowy days, after turning up for form's sake, they vanish into thin air. They wear jackets while doing double time, and when they fly, these *reconnaissance* men burn octane #87 fuel simply because they graduated from the Naval Academy, while we *pilots* make do with alcohol fuel. That's the navy.

The hazard light on the radio pole was on all through the night. I just looked at it, saying to myself that red beacon lights have a certain atmosphere about them, whether it's the running light on a ship or the rear lamp of an express train, not giving the matter a second thought. But it turns out that the commander went missing on his way back from an official trip to Tokyo, and he still hadn't returned, even though it was well past nine. And that was why the light was on all night. The report came in this morning, however, that he made an emergency landing at Suzuka Air Station.

One more carrier bomber crash-landed yesterday, which finally brought their training flights to a halt. Strange to say, the cat stopped meowing, as if in reply. Made me a little superstitious.

Today, a recon student was hit by the propeller of a plane as it taxied onto the apron. He was killed instantly, and as his body was flung away it struck another man who was seriously wounded and presently died in the medical ward. One of them was the ensign who really put us through the wringer because someone wore a shirt during calisthenics. For the most part, we think it was sweet, sweet justice, though we certainly don't say so aloud. There was no denying the general mood: *Take that, you bastard.* The accident was attributed to carelessness, an after-effect of the liberty the recon students were granted yesterday. So an instructor lectured us, "Never let your guard down during liberty. When you are out on an excursion, always remember its purpose. You are getting the rest and relaxation you need in order to fly your aircraft into battle. Don't lapse into intemperance simply because you feel free."

"We're always to blame!" someone said afterwards, in a sulk. "It's our fault that mailboxes are red. And if the utility poles are tall, well, that's our fault too. Everything's our fault. Shit!" Indeed, we reserve officers are blamed for everything. Well, do with us as you please.

We have devised a piece of equipment we call the "W.C. band."

"Hey, give me your band," someone said. I didn't get it at first, but he meant the belt from my judo outfit. And here's why: On top of the four hundred fifty "knee-bends with arm lifts" we did, we run some eight kilometers a day at double time. This only compounds the pain in our muscles. Our legs ache even when we are standing, and we can't squat down in the toilet. So this fellow lashed my judo belt to a steel pipe in the john, and used it to hold his body in position while emptying his bowels. What a brilliant idea! And in short, this is the story of the "W.C. band."

One enemy tank division and two infantry divisions have landed on Luzon. Two more divisions are said to be on standby.

The temperature dropped to six below zero Celsius this morning.

Fujikura's letter

Usa Naval Air Station, Oita Prefecture
January 23, Showa 20 (1945)
Professor E.
Kita-Shirakawa, Kyoto

Professor E.

K. sent me a letter that fills me with envy. He says that, on the spur of the moment, he visited your house in Kyoto wearing his sergeant's uniform, and that you treated him to beer over reminiscences and rumors. He also told me that your family has evacuated to the countryside in Tottori Prefecture. You prepare your own meals now, and you ventured to say that, if it were only the old days come again, you would bring together under your roof all the members of the usual *Manyo* circle—K., Yoshino, Sakai, Kashima, and myself. I felt a catch in my throat as I thought back on those good old days. How did K. look as a sergeant?

It has been eight months since I wrote you. When we moved from Tsuchiura to Izumi last May, I sent you what ought properly be termed a lengthy disclosure of my heart, in reply to which I received only the briefest of notes. To be honest, I concluded that, after all, even *you* are doing nothing more, with respect to this war, than comporting yourself respectably, and consequently, that I am totally forsaken. Disappointed and jaundiced, I have long neglected to write you again, until reading K.'s letter, which gave me the impulse to put pen to paper.

I learned from K. that you said, "I suspect Mr. Fujikura might be agonizing the most. I hope he will manage somehow."

I was genuinely grateful. To put it the old-fashioned way, I thought: Your regard alone is enough for me. Maybe I'm interpreting your feelings to suit my own wishes, but anyway I will not be upset if I don't receive a reply from you.

To tell you the truth, I *am* thinking of "managing somehow." As I see it, Japan has already lost every asset that might have allowed for victory in this war. Saipan fell, the Philippines collapsed. Millions of Japanese remain behind, checkmated, in the southwestern and southeastern theaters, where the enemy has them completely beleaguered and stands poised to launch a counteroffensive. From the enemy's point of view, it must simply be a matter of methodically drawing in the net. As for what it will be like to lose the war, I still can't begin to imagine. The country dismembered, any number of people starving to death, riots erupting one after another, the occupation forces tyrannizing, Kyoto and Yamato in ruins. In the face of all this, any hope of returning to campus might well be shattered, might well prove nothing but a lunatic dream. Still, it's one thing to say it will be a disaster if we lose this war, and quite another to say that, e*rgo,* we will win it. Everybody seems innocently to put these two ideas together, bringing forth, in sum, a kind of awful optimism. But however disastrous it may be, Japan has no choice left but to lose. I just wish we could at least lose with the nation intact, though it looks like I cannot hope for even that.

Professor E.

Our training flights have been on hold for quite some time due to the fuel shortage. For a moment, I hoped against hope that if things go on like this, who knows but that the war might suddenly end while we just mill around, digging holes in the ground or some such thing, with no further worry on my part. I fancied putting on airs and giving Yoshino a smack on the jaw, saying, "Wake up! We're going back to Kyoto!" However, the reality is not so easy, as I just found out. The other day, we were finally compelled to volunteer for the special attack force. We resume flights the day after tomorrow. We will be burning alcohol fuel, a low-grade, dangerous type of fuel that fails to ignite if the temperature inside the cylinders drops a little, causing the propellers to stop in midair.

The general public seems to think that only the bravest men, the men who have unswerving loyalty, ever volunteer for the special attack force, but that was only at the earliest stage. Now that headquarters has fully adopted the tactic, they use our superior officers to recruit volunteers. "Will you step forward?" the officers ask, or "Will you raise your hand?" And at last even a man like me feels compelled to raise his hand, heavy as lead. Ostensibly the decision is voluntary, but psychologically speaking, it's downright coercion. And with that, we give them free rein to choose whomever they want to choose. I will have very little chance of survival if I simply continue to drift along. So I am contemplating some extreme measure to save my life, and my life alone. It is all I ever think about, night and day. Professor, please do not reproach me for being selfish, unless you really do want me to crash into the enemy alongside my comrades. I shall be content if you only consider me an impossible fellow. I have no power to save Sakai and Yoshino. We are already too far apart in our thinking. All I could ever do is make them angry; I could never make them listen. Even Kashima, the man we all would have thought furthest from being a fighter, routinely sends in from the torpedo boat camp in Kawatana (though never, of course, to me) lines like: "You guys come in from the air, I will come in on the water," or "Be that as it may, we must set about preparing for our journey to the other world."

I have thought of various methods. One option is to get myself badly injured in an "accident," to the extent that I won't be able to fly again. But as I observed the results of the accidents on our base, I had to conclude that this plan simply offers too little chance of survival. My second idea supposes that enemy troops land on Formosa or in southern China and build a base. When it is time to make my sortie, I will fly to that base and desert, giving myself up as a prisoner. If I succeed, my survival will be all but guaranteed, and I assume I would be able to return safely to Japan once the war ends. The problem is that unless I have some way to inform the other side of my plan in advance, I will naturally be shot down by their fighters or antiaircraft guns before I ever reach the base. This plan, therefore, has little chance of success. So, I started to give shape to what has been vaguely on my mind ever since I dared choose to be a pilot back at Tsuchiura Naval Air Station. Namely, I am thinking of crash-landing on some island while engaged in a special attack mission. From now on, our sorties should be directed mainly at the Ryukyu Islands or the area around Formosa. As you know, there are a lot of handy little islands along the way, islands with few inhabitants, small garrisons, and poor communications. Or, I started to think, maybe a desert island would do, depending on the circumstances. So I have been collecting maps of the Ryukyu Islands and reading "castaway" stories like *Robinson Crusoe*, studying all the parts that may prove helpful. I will take off, proceeding as usual until we near the island I have chosen, at which point I will feign engine trouble or something like that. First, I will stray from my formation and release the bomb. Then I'll take the thick cushion from the seat and apply it to the instrument panel so as to protect my head on impact. Finally, my belt securely fastened, I will close the throttle and ditch the plane tail first into the water, with landing gear pulled in. Needless to say, the aircraft will go to pieces, and it might end up nose down in the water. But in any case, it will not sink immediately, giving me enough time to unfasten the belt and escape. After that, I should be able to swim to the island. Judging from the present situation, they won't be in any hurry to rescue me (!), even if they do learn about the accident, and nobody will ever know whether or not my plane really had trouble in the air.

I still have some problems to solve, food, for example. But my plan is taking shape quite sensibly along the lines laid out above, and about ninety percent of it is now in place. However, one thing is strange. As the blueprint of my escape plan comes into focus, a certain indefinable emptiness sweeps through my mind. I don't know quite how to explain it, but suppose I somehow manage to survive on the island. There I am, spending my days fishing or whatever, when all of sudden I spot a detachment of the special attack force overhead—my comrades, roaring atop the clouds and heading south. And after they are gone there remains only the sky, absurdly bright and tranquil, and that hollow tint of it vividly strikes my eyes. So far as I can tell, it's not that my conscience is bothering me because what I intend to do is cowardly, and it's not exactly a fear of solitude, either. I fully intend to dodge the pointless death marked out for me here, but when I picture the color of that sky, the prospect of survival also begins to seem dreary. I can do nothing with this strange, empty, enervating void, so I will simply have to root out this feeling.

Actually, we occasionally hear that among the many who make their "Will Die, Will Kill" sorties, there are some who ditch their planes more or less in the way I have in mind, and they survive, marooned on an island somewhere. These men didn't follow a deliberate course of action, or so it seems anyway. They just fell into a funk along the way, and desperately ditched their planes on an impulse. But mine is a calculated move, planned far in advance, and this is doubtless what makes me feel so hollowed out. And now I'm thinking: Setting off in such a frame of mind, I might be impelled by the *opposite* kind of impulse, an impulse that says, "Maybe it's actually easier just to go ahead and die." And thus I may end up meeting Fate with all my comrades, which is not impossible. I expect I will have to suppress that impulse by sheer willpower. I used to be a diffident student. I had my doubts about the value of studying the *Manyoshu* as it was, and now I can't possibly make it my mission to survive in order to work on it further for my comrades. Maybe that partly accounts for the emptiness I feel. I close my eyes, I strain my ears, but from nowhere do I hear a voice saying: "You must live. Don't think about the others. It's all right. You deserve to survive." Needless to say, I am certainly not trying to coax any such words out of you. When you cannot accept this war, when you are poised to take a different path and watch your friends die before your very eyes, it is agony.

However, Professor, I intend to sustain myself and to endure the ordeal of this strange void, and if I am to suffer unspoken accusations, then I will endure them, too. When Japan stages its next big operation, and you hear that I made a sortie and am missing, please conclude that I'm probably alive on some southern island where I ditched my plane. I will wait for the war to end, and surely I will return to Kyoto. Would you welcome me? And if my attempt fails, and you get news that I "died in the line of duty" (?!), then please remember, from time to time, that there was one naval ensign among the men who came under your tutelage who just could not approve of this war, and that he died, rejecting it to the end.

When I write, I always end up producing a long, incoherent letter. I'm sorry about that. But setting aside our struggles, you yourself must be leading a terribly hard life. This might be the last letter I send you till the very day I make my sortie, but please take good care of yourself. And finally, I have a favor to ask of you. When we were stationed in Izumi, we visited, on every outing, a family in Minamata by the name of Fukai. They were very kind to us. The head of the household is Mr. Nobunori Fukai, and he has a daughter called Fukiko. I have already explained my plans, but in our situation nobody knows what the future holds, and if I die and Yoshino survives, I would like you to act as a go-between for Yoshino and this girl.

Miss Fukai appeared to like each of us, though in different ways. In other words, she was vaguely attracted to these brave naval aviation officers with a scholarly air about them. Rationally speaking, I don't want any woman to like me based on an overestimation of my character, and emotionally speaking, she is not exactly my type anyway, though she is certainly beautiful and sweet. So I feigned ignorance of her affections throughout our acquaintance. Yoshino, however, still pines for her, even four months after our leaving Izumi. I know this perfectly well, as

I have watched him closely ever since I became convinced of his feelings while we were still at Izumi. He would never admit it, because he believes he is going to crash into the enemy and die, but he broods over Miss Fukai most unhandsomely, whenever he is alone. In any case, it's not as if I were giving away to a friend a woman I really love. Instead, I'm just a backseat driver, I suppose. Anyway, I wanted somebody else to know about this, in case the roll of the dice leaves Yoshino alive and me dead. And if the match should be made through the good offices of Professor E., that would be highly desirable. Indeed, perfect. And if there really is another world beneath the sod, I shall be watching the couple from there, with satisfaction. That is why I'm asking you to keep this in mind.

With best wishes. I will post this letter tomorrow, the 24th, in Beppu, during our excursion.

Usa Naval Air Station

JANUARY 25 (CONTINUED FROM YOSHINO'S DIARY)

Our training flights resumed today.

We use alcohol fuel, which takes considerable nerve. I tossed and turned last night, my sleep interrupted frequently by dreams. No doubt anxiety about the fuel is at the bottom of it.

A number of carrier attack bombers and carrier bombers are making trial runs in front of the field headquarters. Three Type-96 carrier bombers particularly got into my brain, as they kept up a good roar right nearby. I had to endure a constant pressure in my head, which grew heavy, as if I were holding the whole world on top of it. It wasn't much of a thrill.

Mutual flight. I climbed into the rear seat of Ensign W.'s plane. Truly, it's been a long while since I last flew. The cloud index was eight. The wind was strong, with a velocity of some ten meters per second, and the direction shifted frequently from west to northwest, and then to the north. But how rusty my skills are! First, I forgot about the flap. I couldn't attend to the tabs. The winds only made matters worse. The plane bounced up and down and waggled, speed fluctuating wildly. I got nauseated. How pathetic! It wasn't just me, though.

"The damn thing wouldn't go my way! I had no idea I'd so completely lost my touch!" That's about all you heard as everyone tottered out of the planes, quite beside themselves. I asked what route they took, but no one seemed to have the slightest idea. We were all soundly rebuked, but I really wish the officers wouldn't lecture us about our deteriorating performance when they've kept us grounded for two and a half months. The recon students enjoy two flights a day, morning and evening, and on regular fuel, too, while we carrier attack bombers attached to the special attack force fly every other day, and on alcohol. Nobody blinks at this bizarre state of affairs. It is not fair to compare our skills to theirs. But we will catch up to them, alcohol fuel or no. And we will learn enough to take us to the place where we mean to die.

Had a bath at 1900. The water was good and hot. I scrubbed my body with soap, which I haven't done for some time. As I got out, I gazed into the mirror and found myself looking pretty grave. *You cocky bastard, loosen up a little!* I said to myself, and I made some silly faces, pulling my cheeks, and poking out my lips, until my clownish mug made me a little melancholy. I heard somebody laughing. Through the bathroom window I could see the moon, hanging warped in the sky. I ate an orange, smoked a Hikari, and finished a leftover soda, and then sank into a sound sleep.

Flew in the morning. I'm beginning to get a sense of the air again. The winds were light. The thin, silver line of the Yakkan River, the Sea of Suo, the Kunisaki Peninsula, Beppu Bay off to the south—it all looked hazy, giving me the feeling of spring. I've managed to make a bit of room in my heart to enjoy the bird's-eye view. The rain came in this afternoon, putting an end to flights for the day. It kept up well into the night.

During the course on combat tactics we learned that the Ginga turned out to be pretty useless, falling well short of expectations. It was a real letdown. The Type-1 land-based attack bomber earned the nickname "Cigar" for its shape, but nowadays, seeing as how it so readily catches fire, everybody just calls it a "Match." But even so, some Ginga crews purportedly say they prefer the Type-1, as their plane has proved so difficult to maintain and is forever getting them into accidents. This account accords with what we so often witnessed at Izumi.

The U.S. has occupied the air base at Clark Field, north of Manila, and at the end of January a total of some two hundred enemy warships and transports arrived at this strategic zone in the Philippines. I doubt whether we actually have two hundred aircraft left in all the Philippines. The situation is such that even if every single Japanese plane plunges into an enemy vessel and sinks it, we are still outnumbered. They say we now possess fewer than five aircraft carriers, and this figure includes our smaller auxiliary carriers. None of them ever puts out to sea, though, as fuel has to be conserved, and the crews have yet to complete their training. Only a few weeks ago we sat through a lecture on carrier takeoff and landing protocols. At the time I thought the lecture pointless, and indeed, the navy is shot through with hit-or-miss training and willy-nilly strategies. America is said to possess some eighty aircraft carriers, and they are about to commission three new forty-five thousand ton class vessels capable of carrying medium attack bombers. Well, we will mark out a line of defense along the shore of mainland Japan, and *there* we will annihilate the enemy, at a blow; we no longer need any aircraft carriers. *That's* the logic on our side, but it all sounds like sour grapes to me. I hear our Japanese comrades are struggling to complete air bases in Formosa and in southern Kyushu, but with hoes and pickaxes they are making extremely slow progress, whereas the U.S. military can complete the same task in three days using its bulldozers and dump trucks. Also, I hear the signs indicate that a major enemy task force will advance toward mainland Japan within two weeks. As for our situation, it looks like mass production of the Ryusei, the Shiden, and the Renzan won't get into gear until May or June.

"When May rolls around they'll probably tell us 'not until July or August,'" the tactics instructor said, spilling the beans, evidently half in despair. He spared us the usual talk about "that's why you must steel yourself with do-or-die resolution, blah-blah-blah." Felt all the more uncanny for it.

There are three young trainees who predict the future using a planchette. About once a week, we call them in and ask all kinds of questions. You have to be serious, though, if you actually expect an answer. They position a plate atop three interlocked chopsticks and summon the spirits. The chopsticks rattle, the plate flutters, and with that the prophesying begins. So far they've managed to find a few lost items, but today they prophesied that the greater East Asian war will end on April 23, Showa 22 (1947), with a victory for Japan. Incidentally, there is talk that a freak cow was born in Hiroshima, with a human face and the body of a beast. I saw the picture, and indeed, the creature has a very human look about it, with its high nose, like a pensive old man. The body, however, is undoubtedly a cow's. In any case, this freak cow purportedly spoke our language, and it said, just before dying, "After losing three battles, Japan will greet the end of the war in brilliant triumph." Sakai, by the way, repeated the words of Admiral Saneyuki Akiyama at the Battle of Tsushima in 1905, which he stumbled across in some book: "Should Japan and America go to war, I can keep us in the running even if I lose Kyushu." For his part, Fujikura is as sour as vinegar. Obviously, the freak cow and the planchette are simply too absurd for him. I myself can't see how the present war situation could lead to a Japanese victory in April of Showa 22. Still, I can't quite bring myself, like Fujikura, to sweep these prophecies aside as fakes, or as mere superstition.

Anyway, I guess I shouldn't be wasting time with matters like these. Whether Japan wins or loses, we will already have perished. Suppose a man is stopping up holes in some embankment, one by one, when the murky water starts coming through. The moment he loses his faith is the moment everything washes away.

We flew yesterday. Alcohol fuel isn't as bad as I had feared, and I'm gaining confidence. The airflow is good, and it's easy to pull into the approach path. I fluffed it once, though, during my second flight. The movements of hands and feet are organically linked, and, given the speed at which everything must happen during takeoffs and landings, you can blow the whole thing with one little mistake.

"Come on, now. You'll have to fly solo soon," said Lt.jg S., repeatedly.

It started to snow. When you're up in the air, the flakes strike your face with tremendous speed, and that, together with the pressure of the wind, hurt my throat a little. Once the snow began to pile up, flights were canceled, and we were placed on the Saturday schedule.

Liberty today. Yesterday's snow froze over, and there was a distinct chill in the air. My shoes kept slipping on the ice, which made it a nuisance to walk. Three submarines lay at anchor in the Sea of Beppu, together with a submarine tender. One of them was huge, its gunwale curving up at the bow, which made it look more like a destroyer when viewed head-on. On the train we happened across a crowd of submariners. Their skin was brown with grime, and they stank to high heaven. Many more were at the inn in Kamegawa, and every one of them stank. I have nothing but respect for these men who have only just returned from a long and trying operation. Still, I have to say it, they really *do* stink. Because the inn was thronged with crewmen from the submarines, guys from our base, and also civilians, men and women bathed together. Well, the young women are certainly bold in Kyushu. It was embarrassing for me, and I felt awkward and strange.

From the train, I saw a big snowman in a stretch of snow on the western side of the tracks, dingy from the smoke of the locomotives.

The situation at the front in the Philippines is just retreat after retreat. U.S. troops reportedly charged into Manila on the 3rd, and I fear the city may be completely in their hands by now. The newspapers keep up their constant cry, "We have caused the enemy immense distress!" But the men at the front know they keep retreating without hurting the Americans much, the newsmen know it, and Imperial Headquarters knows it, too. In short, the whole country keeps saying "We have caused the enemy immense distress!" but nobody believes a word of it. I hear they are making bamboo spears round the clock in Tokyo, so as to inspire hostility toward the enemy and boost morale. At the same time, no underground bunkers have yet been constructed, either for the evacuation of civilians, or to protect our arsenal. The menu at Senbiki-ya has dwindled down to one item: *oyako-donburi* with a disproportionate amount of onion.

On the train back, we had a chat with an engineering outfit lately returned from the India-Burma border. All it takes is a few cigarettes to set them blabbing out everything they know. I was disgusted, even though we started it. The train was twenty minutes late, so we ran all the way from Yanagiga-ura

Station. I slipped twice on the snow. Fujikura and Sakai slipped, too. Two *Manyo* poems about snow came to mind.

> Snow fell heavily
> In our town of Asuka.
> Only later will it reach
> The ancient town of Ohara.

> If only I were
> With my dear husband,
> How delightful it would be
> To watch the falling snow!

FEBRUARY 14

I pulled first shift as probational assistant officer of the day. Intelligence came in that an enormous enemy task force, with forty or fifty aircraft carriers at its core, had left its anchorage in the Marianas. We prepared for battle at six in the evening. Then, at 0400 this morning, we were placed on Defense Condition 2. The situation grew tense.

Afternoon flights were canceled. In order to clear the way for fifty Gingas to advance to this base, we moved the carrier attack bombers we use for training out to the off-field hangars. I wheeled aircraft #3 out, puncturing its tire as I forced it to taxi over the rough surface.

The 701st, 501st, and 708th Air Units stationed at this base are all special attack force units, and the petty officers of the 708th, who bunk in the drill hall, are beginning to show unmistakable kinks in their personality as they face death. Last night and again tonight, they got drunk and came over to the barracks, swagger sticks in hand, and told us that, seeing as how they are going to die tomorrow, we should show them a little more consideration. They repeated the phrase "We are going to die tomorrow" like blockheads, and started a scuffle with the whole lot of us students. It is no easy task to make good use of men like this, while leading them into death.

The flag of the Ohka bomber group flies next to the windsock at the field headquarters. Also up is a banner bearing the motto: "Reason above error. Tradition above reason. Power above tradition. Providence over all." As we were told a while ago, the Ohka is the Japanese answer to the V-1 rocket, a small craft with stubby wings. It rides in the bay of a Type-1 land-based attack bomber until it is time to launch, at which point it leaves the plane, sending the signal · · · — ·, or "Period," and then it's farewell to this world. It doesn't matter if you run into trouble, there's no coming back for a second try. The moment an Ohka leaves the mother plane everything reaches its end. The same goes for special attack force pilots. But the Ohka men are gloomy and warped, while the Ginga crews are sunny, and the crews of the Type-1's just hang loose.

At night, the Gingas flew in and landed, one by one. In keeping with the blackout order, only the red hazard lights burned, as if to suggest the turn of fate.

FEBRUARY 16

No advance by the enemy task force yesterday. The sortie was canceled. No flights at all.

During flight training today, news poured in. Carrier-based planes raided the Kanto area, and Yokohama and Kono-ike Air Stations are both presently under attack. Ten land-based attack bombers were sent up at Kono-ike. The capital appears to be suffering blow after blow. Chichi-jima and Iwo-jima also suffered raids.

About twenty Type-96s advanced to this base from Toyohashi. Having mobilized some fifty land-based attack bombers, and an equal number of Gingas, Usa is set to become the largest single rendezvous point for special attack force aircraft. Still, the Ohka Units will not go out just yet. Obviously, they intend to draw the enemy in closer. In the early evening, eighteen Gingas took off, headed for Kanoya in Kagoshima Prefecture.

Some of us are to receive accelerated training, myself included. I thought a full year would pass before I died, but it looks now as if it will be a matter of months.

FEBRUARY 18

Got up at five and prepared to meet the enemy planes. The 501st Air Unit has been on standby since midnight. The motors were kept running all through the night. I felt the roar of the propellers in my gut. If I don't brace for it, eyes wide open, I get nauseated. At ground level, the air is heavy and the resistance is stiff, and if you rev up the engines too much you overwork the pistons, which eventually cease to fire normally. Making a racket—pow! pow! pow!—they actually inhibit the spin of the propellers. The maximum limit at ground level is a zero millimeter boost. Zero out the lever and your eardrums all but burst.

At around noon, the crews assembled outside the field headquarters. The order to launch was issued at the report that the enemy had been sighted offshore at Cape Muroto and also at Ariake Bay. Our men will rally at Kanoya Air Station, and, a few hours later, proceed on their special attack missions. We exchanged farewell cups of water, and lined up at an angle along the airstrip to see the planes off, waving our caps. Eighteen Gingas bore the men away. Some waved their caps from the cockpit, others gave salutes. Those who took the trouble to taxi toward us before gliding on to the takeoff point, or who stood up in the front reconnoiterers' seat, all appeared to be our predecessors from the 13th Class, men from Keio, Waseda, and Tokyo Universities. As they left the ground, the men thrust the tips of their hands from the signalman's seat and waved to us, vigorously. The hands grew smaller and smaller as the planes gathered speed and quickly slipped out of sight. A tightness gripped my throat. Afterwards, we dispersed the remaining aircraft.

FEBRUARY 22

Turned out to be a disappointment. Four days have passed. Nothing happened.

On the 19th, we watched as the Gingas returned. We did hear reports that our side sank two enemy aircraft carriers, and also some battleships and cruisers, but I have to say these successes are insignificant. We never employed our main force after all. If we lay onto a mere handful of aircraft the responsibility of determining the nation's fate, as if in an effort to put them to their best and highest use, then inevitably our strategy will be a passive one.

The enemy took a full swing before turning back. After receiving reports that their task force was moving, we have heard nothing at all. Ten thousand hostile men landed on Iwo-jima. Should the airfields on this island fall into American hands, Tokyo and Osaka will be within range of whole fleets of enemy fighters and bombers.

Last night's snow piled up nearly ten centimeters high, but it's the wet kind. The sun is strong and the air is warm. It's a fair spring day, and I want to strip down a bit and bask in it. The season has arrived when (as a *Manyo* poet has it) "the brackens / By the waterfall / Burst into leaf." G. says that the dandelions may be out. The larks are already singing. *Kyushu isn't half bad,* I said to myself, *and it's not bad to be alive, either.*

We had a snowball fight. This snow sure packs hard. We wrestled each other, full of energy, and made a big snowman. Afterwards we dug up some fresh snow to eat with coffee syrup. Delicious.

Last night, the Ginga men went on a bender, guzzling that rationed sake called "Taiheiyo" ("The Pacific Ocean"). As they wound down, they flocked together and wept. This afternoon, one by one, they departed for Izumi, kicking up snow as they rose from the airstrip. We saw them off.

For the first time in ages, I got a letter from my aunt in Kobe. Brandishing the envelope, which bore her name, Hatsuko Miyoshi, in ink, the instructor demanded fifty sen. (We get fined every time we receive a letter from a woman.) "No," I protested. "It's from my aunt. She's fifty-eight years old. I just contributed five yen the other day, when I hung my plane up on a pothole. Come on, just give me a break, will you?" He didn't. I had to pay. My aunt says some one hundred B-29s raided Kobe on the 4th of this month, inflicting heavy damage. The Miyoshi residence, however, was safe.

Fujikura is dead.

It happened during training this morning. After I landed, Fujikura climbed into plane #6 for its third flight. Right after takeoff, though, he lifted the nose too high, sending the plane into a stall, and in a flash he had crashed, left wing first. I ran out to the spot. The control stick was embedded in his face, his eyeballs dangled down around his lips, and the back of his head, all whitish, was split open. He was dead, without much bleeding. The impact threw the engine ten meters away from the fuselage. The main left wing had been sheared away by the rocks, and the tail was shattered. At around 1027 on the morning of March 1, Showa 20, Fujikura ended his twenty-five years of life. Senior Aviation Petty Officer B., also on board, was rushed off to the medical ward on a rescue unit stretcher. His face was swollen to twice its normal size, and he suffered deep gashes, but it looks like he will survive. Murase and I stayed behind to tend to Fujikura's body, while everybody else resumed their flights in the afternoon. Sakai stopped by later. After dinner, we held a wake for Fujikura in the lounge.

The winds blew in from the east today, bringing spring with them. We all took off our uniforms and changed into light and airy fatigues. Fujikura had been wearing a snow-white, open-neck shirt at morning assembly, and the image of it remains in my mind. I try not to let my feelings overcome me, but tears fill my eyes as scattered reminiscences of Fujikura flood my mind: The man who smuggled oranges in his gaiters and shared them with us on a day when we were allowed visitors but no food or drink back at Otake Naval Barracks. The man who, during our farewell party at the Fukais' house, sang, with a straight face, a song titled "Draw the Lamp and Catch the Lice," all the while gazing up at the ceiling. The man who so sternly rebuked me for having struck a petty officer by the swimming pool. The man who taught me the difference between a blue flag iris and a rabbit-ear iris at Kutai Temple during the *Manyo* trip we made in the spring of Showa 18 (after which we engaged in a day-long debate as to whether asthmaweed and horseweed are actually the same).

I don't know how to handle the notices to his family, to Professors O. and E., and to the Fukais. In the meantime, I at least have to notify Kashima in Kawatana.

He had to die sooner or later, and in his case it's not quite right to say he must regret having fallen before ever realizing his wish to go to the front. We had few opportunities during the last month or two to sit down and talk, even when we made an outing. As a matter of fact, Fujikura rather seemed to want to avoid talking, and it appeared that something had been troubling him. My guess is that he just couldn't reconcile himself to the idea of embarking on a special attack mission, and that he agonized, unable to distract himself from it all, day after day. If that's the case, I really should consider this accident a blessing in disguise, as an unlooked-for death took him before he ever had to face the real anguish.

Rest in peace, Fujikura. I, too, was utterly exhausted today, both mentally and physically. I decided to excuse myself early from the wake to get some sleep, so as to be sharp during training flights tomorrow.

Tunneling work. We're digging an air-raid shelter in the hillside on the other side of the river. There will be eight chambers in total, about a hundred meters deep, with passages connecting them. A medical ward, a barracks, and corridors, all of it underneath the earth. Someday we will live in this hole. The soil is soft here, so we can dig out as much as four meters a day, but ten workers spoil the air all too quickly. They really need to see to it that this space has sufficient ventilation if they ever mean to use it as a medical ward.

We spent half the day yesterday cremating Fujikura's body in a stretch of pine trees along the Yakkan River. At five in the afternoon we gathered his ashes. Obviously the fire burned too hot, as the bones had crumbled into tiny pieces. We gathered them up carefully. Fujikura is treated as having died in the line of duty, so he will receive a posthumous promotion to the rank of lieutenant junior grade.

Because he majored in Japanese literature, Sakai was asked to compose a poem in tribute to the deceased. He brooded for a while and came up with what sounds like a haiku: "So-and-so / Gathering ashes / On the day of the Doll's Festival." He says he just can't find the right words for the first line. In the end, we agreed we had better pick out something from the *Manyoshu*, and as we were browsing through it we received a telegram from Kashima. Coincidentally, he had sent in a *Manyo* poem, too.

I had no way to go and see him.
May clouds gather over Ishikawa

So that I can, at least, gaze at them
And cherish his memory.

We also chose a poem on Hitomaro from the elegies in the second volume, and copied it down in ink on a sheet of the lined paper that the navy uses. We laid this out for Fujikura, along with Kashima's telegram. Some of the men offered navel oranges, eight of which were rationed to each of us today. Fujikura's parents are supposed to arrive tomorrow.

March 15

While I've been neglecting this diary, the river has risen, and the cherry blossoms on the base are now one-fifth in bloom. The larks chirp constantly, wheeling up and down over the barley fields. Fujikura's accident slides into the past. Fortunately, we are blessed with a capacity for oblivion.

From the cockpit I enjoy a little world of spring. Our flight today was longer than usual, so we carried along a urine bag. It wasn't easy at first; I wasn't used to it and had to work myself up into a weird posture. But in the end it felt good. Below me lay green fields of barley, and I saw the white wakes of the small fishing boats. The air is somewhat hazy. I felt a bit like looping the loop.

However, the Type-97 carrier attack bomber offers nothing to protect the pilot besides a seatbelt. We do stow a parachute under us like a cushion, with the ripcord tied to the seat. But as the instructors have indicated ("Listen, guys," they say, "don't expect it to open"), this arrangement rarely works as it should if you have to bail out. The windshield sits right in front of your face. If you bang to a halt, breaking the landing gear or something like that, your forehead slams into the glass, killing you for sure. Come to think of it, it's amazing they train us in these planes, and with defective fuel to boot.

When we wrapped up for the day, we were told to expect a Sunday schedule tomorrow. This means a day of liberty. After that, operations will keep us confined to base until May 1st. We returned to the barracks, quacking like ducks. There we learned that Osaka was raided last night by some ninety B-29s. The newspaper ran a picture: A rainstorm of firebombs cascaded down, flames trailing along behind them. Supposing the payload of a B-29 to be ten tons, and judging by the range from which this raid was launched, for each household in Osaka there must have been four, five, or even ten firebombs. Abeno, Tenno-ji, and Sumiyoshi Wards were completely incinerated. The damage yesterday, as well as the devastation of the March 10 raid on Tokyo, is said to match that of the Great Kanto Earthquake of 1923.

I'm getting concerned about my family. And I'm also concerned about the civilian population in general, wondering whether or not they will manage to pull through when they are hard-pressed to meet even the barest needs and begin to doubt their own prospects. I have a feeling that if we start falling apart now, there will be no stopping it, and if that's the case, I don't know what it is we're dying for.

The number of B-29s our side reportedly shot down: a mere eleven.

MARCH 22

An order to evacuate immediately came in on the 18th. We flew to Miho Air Station in Shimane Prefecture and just got back today. Reveille was at five thirty on the 18th, and with it came the call to man our stations. We formed in front of the field headquarters and stood by. Twenty of our land-based attack bombers took off shortly on a mission. A report had come in that an enemy task force of three regular aircraft carriers and two auxiliary carriers had appeared to the south of Cape Ashizuri, about two hundred nautical miles from this base.

At 0730, we returned to the barracks for breakfast, half of us at a time. At around 0930 news came in that our attack bombers had set one of the enemy carriers on fire. On the heels of this report came another, indicating that one hundred twenty Grummans were circling over the city of Oita. We were certain that it was our turn at last to make a sortie, but instead we received the order to evacuate to Miho, together with all our aircraft. They said we might encounter Grummans en route, in which case we should fall into air combat, or, as circumstances dictated, crash our planes into them. We wrote out brief farewell notes in a hurry, and at around 1210, thirty-six carrier attack bombers and thirty carrier bombers formed up and set out for Miho. All landed safely, except for one bomber, which straggled behind and made an emergency landing along the way. Miho Naval Air Station is situated at a lovely spot near Lake Shinji and Nakano-umi, with a fine view of snow-capped Mt. Daisen.

It was right after we took off that Usa was hit. On our return four days after the raid the survivors told us how, at around one o'clock, they suddenly heard a strange roar. Four Grummans popped into view, already in a nosedive. They strafed the hangars and the Type-1 land attack bombers, diving to within ten meters of the ground. They came in so low they almost grazed the tails of the Type-1s before pulling out and flying away. They were very nimble indeed, we were told. From the vicinity of the field headquarters, our side fired 7.7 millimeter machine guns like all fury, but the 7.7 is nothing in the face of the enemy's 13.7 millimeter guns. What really put up stiff resistance was an army aircraft called the Hien, which engaged the enemy in a three-cornered dogfight. It fought splendidly throughout the raid. Still, the flock of Grummans got away more or less unscathed. They circled leisurely as they gathered, and then they flew away. Following this came more attacks, at around two, and then again at half past three. The enemy planes had totally free rein as they flew in from the southwest out of a glaring sun. Their rocket artillery had the Type-1s blazing away, one after another, the hangars were in flames, the Ohka was never able to get off the ground, the switchboard failed, and we had a crop of martyrs. Those who had set out, leaving behind their farewell notes, survived, every one of them, while those who stayed were killed. By the time we came back, all the bodies had been cremated on the riverbank in fires stoked with airplane fuel. Their ashes were already laid out. The men returning from Miho tore up the notes they had left, with a wry grin.

I went out to the airfield for a walk. Few Tenzans escaped the bullets. I made my way to the end of the runways. Ripe horsetails covered the fields, which gave off the fresh scent of spring grass. What appeared to be a local farmer's wife and her daughter were heading home, carrying a coarsely woven basket full of horsetails.

"It's all right. Can I help you?" I asked, concerned that they might think I'd come to shoo them away. "Thank you," they said, "but we've already called it a day. It looks like rain." Indeed, it soon began to mist. I stood alone on the empty airfield, gazing from a distance at the land-based attack bombers, with their wings crumpled by rocket fire, and at the burnt-out engines that lay scattered around, abandoned. A feeling of desolation overcame me, as if I were on an ancient battlefield.

The banner of the Ohka's Nonaka Unit is gone. "Glory to the Sutra of the Lotus of the Supreme Law," it had said, borrowing a phrase from the Nichiren Buddhists. I was told that the unit had advanced to Kanoya, from which place they are today supposed to mount an attack on two enemy task forces, three hundred sixty nautical miles south of the base. The Ohka men always had an air of gloom about them. On the other hand, the crews of the land-based attack bombers that carry them possess the hearts of lions. Their valor is unparalleled. Sometimes I think I could never match them in a million years of effort. About a dozen Type-1s will set out in the morning, each hugging an Ohka. The wear-and-tear on the mother planes is extreme. On any given raid, half of them are shot down, and the remainder hobbles back after releasing their Ohkas, perforated by bullets. The men eat lunch and set out again, hugging another Ohka. A few hours later a few of them return, with still more bullet holes. The men never crow about their exploits or demand any special consideration. They simply rest for a spell and take to the skies again, toward evening. Until all of them are lost.

It's hard to say which is the more trying, to be the Ohka attacker who sorties never to come back, or to be the attack bomber pilot who carries him. But surely it is no ordinary thing, or so it seems to me, to keep setting out and coming back, like a pilot on some commuter run, until you die.

Our comrades on Iwo-jima have finally perished, in the last ditch effort. It happened at midnight on March 17, I hear. Reports say they killed or wounded seventy-three percent of the enemy's landing force, thirty three thousand men in total, and that they earned us a precious month to prepare for the defense of mainland Japan. The question is whether or not this is the whole story. What did we do to assist the desperate fight that the officers and men made on that island? Could it be that all we really managed to give them was a pep talk, sent in by radio? Isn't the bottom line that we left them in the lurch, without being able to do anything about their situation? At times I think that their fate will be ours also.

March 24

Reveille at 0530. The enemy has attacked Okinawa. An order was given to seven carrier attack bombers to stand ready. The time for us to make our special attack mission finally nears.

The Ohka attacks of the Jinrai Unit failed, with more than 500 Grummans intercepting them. Not one of our fighter planes, sent along for cover, returned. The leader of the raid, Lieutenant Commander Goro Nonaka, died in action. I hear the enemy has given the Ohka the code name BAKA, or fool. I really wish we could somehow show them what the determined soul of a fool is like. I simply don't know what to say.

At four o'clock, the commander addressed us in the lecture hall. But enough already about the "national crisis" and the "sacred cause," we will do what we are supposed to do, without all the talk. Who granted the recon students those excessive flights? Who gave them fuel, granted them a homecoming leave after graduation, and got us in this mess? If only our commanders had allowed us even one hundred hours in the air, we would be much less anxious, ready to embark without a moment's notice. We are resigned to do our duty, green though we may be, but not out of loyalty to the military clique in the Imperial Navy. I take to heart what somebody declared after our sumo match.

MARCH 26

American troops have begun landing on the Kerama Islands. Five battleships and twenty destroyers are blasting away at Okinawa, and their main task force seems to be positioned in the eastern waters. The surviving crewmen from our Type-1 group have all set out. Word is that a standby order was also given to the Ginga and Tenzan Units.

The newspaper carried an article about the Shincho Special Attack Force that assaulted the U.S. fleet at its anchorage in Ulithi. The article doesn't come right out and say so, but it looks like these attacks involved "human torpedoes" fired from submarines. More than half of the crewmen on those torpedoes had once been student reserves. Do the officers from the Naval Academy still regard us as monkeys?

At lunchtime, I received a letter from my father. Learned that our house was safe. A great relief.

This afternoon, we went out to Yokkaichi on air defense operations. If you walk around to the back of the operations area and climb over a rise, you see a dreamscape, a beautiful fold of hills. Overlapping mountains melt into the spring mist in the distance, and the knolls roll off into orchards. Houses with red plum blossoms, hemp fields, pine woods. Tall pampas grass glows in the sun. Bush warblers twitter as they toss freely about, not in the least bit wary of human beings. Along the branch of a buttonwood tree, a bunting basks in the mild sun. The oleasters already bear fruit, though it is not yet ripe. The Yabakei Gorge is probably a ways back in this direction. The water quivers as loach swim in the rice fields. At the base, too, schools of crucian carp and roach teem in the ditches by the field headquarters. For some reason, the contrast between the natural tranquility of these scenes and the fierce desperation of battle seems so unreal.

APRIL 3

Last night, the Wake Squadron of the Go-oh Unit was ordered to make its first sortie. Lieutenant Fujii of the 10th Class (from the University of Tokyo) will lead the carrier attack bombers, and Lt.jg Ennamiji of the 13th Class (from Waseda University) will lead the carrier bombers. Two carrier bomber pilots from our class, Ensigns Ueno and Sugimoto, will also join the mission. Ueno is from Senshu University, and Sugimoto from Keio. Not a single name of a Naval Academy graduate appears on the list. The attack force consists entirely of reserve officers.

After the announcement, Lieutenant Fujii invited me to his room for a drink. He was outraged at the dirty tactics of the Academy graduates. Until very recently he had been in service overseas, and he was assigned to this station in order to get some rest. I can't blame him for being infuriated at the orders. Apparently it's pretty common practice in other units, too, for Academy graduates to stay behind on the pretext that they have to conserve their crews and aircraft. Baffling things happen in the navy.

At seven this morning, Lieutenant Fujii emerged, a new headband on his forehead and a saber in his hand, and climbed into his plane. It is painted green, and had been wiped clean. Not a word of complaint from him today. His last remark was, "Hug the earth and fall, each one of you."

The crews had plucked sprigs from cherry trees and peach trees, and now placed them on the recon seats, or else attached them to their aviation caps. Next came the trial runs. The deafening roar seemed to overwhelm our emotions. I couldn't hear a thing. The planes eased into a glide and formed on the apron. Shortly, Lieutenant Fujii stood up on the recon seat and raised his hand high. And with that, the men took off, heading either for Kushira or Kokubu, in Kagoshima. Some looked cheerful, while others had gone pale from the tension. Then all we could see were their hands, waving briskly from the planes, which slipped out of sight one by one. I pray they will successfully reach their targets; there is nothing else to pray for. I couldn't maintain my composure at all as I waved my cap to see them off.

And yet obviously I still consider it "somebody else's affair" as I watch these men fly away. Apparently, that's just how it goes. A little after half past seven this evening, during study session, Lt.jg T. dropped by the deck, his high boots making their percussive sounds. I looked up and noticed that he bore a small slip of paper in his hand. All of a sudden, my cheeks blazed. He was here to read the list of men named to the second special attack force. A hush enveloped the hall. The lieutenant read the list aloud, casually.

"Ensign Ikushima, Ensign Shirozaki, Ensign Furuichi, Ensign Sakai—"

There was a pause.

"These four men shall prepare themselves to depart at seven tomorrow morning."

The men whose names had not been called puffed out sighs of relief. I immediately looked at Sakai. Shirozaki stood next to him. Sakai was stiff in the face and upper body, as if electrified, and Shirozaki, tough sumo wrestler though he is, flushed red and went completely rigid. We needed to break the news to Furuichi, as he was out of the room. The men were granted a special overnight pass, which amounted to tacit permission to go out and whore. But even those who had been blossoming in that area didn't dare leave the base tonight. At once, we prepared to drink to them. All are from the carrier bomber divisions. Lt.jg Tsuchiya is said to be leading the squadron.

Sakai came unglued and was so beside himself that at first I couldn't look him squarely in the face. But after an hour or so, everyone, Sakai included, gradually started to loosen up. One fellow tried to compose a farewell haiku over a cup of sake, another started to write a goodbye note, still another stowed his gear.

"How do you write the characters for 'riantly'?" asked the man writing the note. Shirozaki stood up, saying, "I'm gonna take a shit first," and disappeared. Before long, Furuichi returned, panting for breath.

I diluted some coffee syrup with hot water to make a good strong cup of the stuff. I carried it in to Sakai, who was writing a sheaf of letters to his family, to K., to Kashima, and to our professors back in Kyoto. He sipped the coffee appreciatively and said, "I wrote my farewell poem." It went:

This same path
You shall follow
In a storm of petals.

"You're telling me not to wait much longer, aren't you?"
I said.

"Well, it's not that exactly, but . . . Fujikura went first.
You third. I don't know what will become of Kashima, but, you
know . . . well, follow me. Doesn't have to be immediately."

"You see, that is what you're telling me."

Sakai had regained enough spirit to share a laugh with me.

Went to bed a little past eleven. Slept in flight suits.
Those who were chosen for this mission snored themselves into
a deep sleep.

Today's war results: Sank one aircraft carrier, two cruisers,
two destroyers, and four more ships of types unknown. Sank or
damaged fifteen ships in total.

APRIL 5

Yesterday's sortie was canceled due to rain.

It's clear and sunny today. The cherry trees on the base
are in full bloom. The men looked glamorous as they had their
pictures taken under the blossoms, their cheeks rosy from a cer-
emonial cup of sake. Only two nights ago they looked so rigid,
their faces distorted. But now, this morning, they all wore calm,
beautiful expressions. This mission will involve twenty-three
carrier attack bombers and eight carrier bombers. Every one of
the men is radiant with youth.

We assembled, and, after a brief, conventional ceremony,
were dismissed. Sakai gestured to me, as if to say, "Excuse me,

please," and ran toward his plane. In the fierce wash of the pro-peller, he ducked to dodge the antenna, his left hand shielding the sprig of a peach tree that his comrades had tucked into the back of his jacket, and then climbed into his seat. At seven o'clock, the lead plane left the apron, with Sakai following five minutes later. As he gazed back at the men on the ground, his face suddenly took on a tearful look. He let go of the control stick and hastily put on his goggles. His feelings resonated in my heart, clear and painful.

Departure. The men glided down the airstrip, gather-ing speed, and flawlessly lifted off. Soon they were mere dots against a blue sky. By seven thirty, all of the first and second groups had finished taking off.

The situation on Okinawa seems to be dire. They say that two airfields are already in enemy hands. Purportedly, the U.S. has deployed fourteen hundred vessels for its operations around Okinawa. I simply don't know whether Japan has any chance at all of recovering, or to what extent the answer rests on the shoulders of Sakai and other pilots like him. But after los-ing two friends, Fujikura and Sakai, I believe I am ready to die, with composure, at any moment.

APRIL 6

At around half past two, I was calibrating the compass at the airfield when word came in of a radio message from our special attack crews. They set off from Kushira at fifteen-minute inter-vals, four planes at a time, starting at around eleven o'clock. It looks like all the special attack aircraft that were on standby at Kushira and Kokubu, and also on Formosa, converged in an avalanche directed at enemy vessels around Okinawa. Army aircraft joined in, too. It is called Operation Kikusui, Number 1.

There is talk that battleships, including the *Yamato*, have set sail for Okinawa, carrying enough fuel only for a one-way trip.

"I've made a successful raid."

"I'm about to make my charge."

"A special providence watches over me. I will now crash into the enemy battleship."

Messages like these came in, one after another. I don't know which was from Sakai, but I'm sure he carried out his mission honorably. If they made successful attacks in those coffee grinders they had to fly, then indeed, there's no other word for it other than "special providence."

Today, early in the morning, Murase, Tahira, and Fujiwara, men from the carrier attack bomber division, joined Ito, from the carrier bomber division, to launch an attack as members of the third Go-oh Unit.

"Now, please excuse me for going first," Ito said as he left the deck, and then added, somewhat jocularly, "The next time the cherry trees blossom, let it be in a peaceful Japan. Really." Probably he couldn't find any other way to express his emotions.

With Shirozaki and Murase gone, the elite sumo team of the 14th class at Usa is destroyed. Five men set out so far from the carrier attack bomber division. I still remain, unchosen.

The temperature dropped low today, with chilly winds blowing. Toward evening, the crews slated to sortie tomorrow visited Usa Shrine.

Lieutenant Commander N., the chief flight officer from our Izumi days, the man we all called the "long-nosed goblin of Kurama," has been posted here as commanding officer of the 722nd Air Unit. He appears whenever our comrades set out, to see off his fledglings.

The fourth Go-oh Unit went out today. Six carrier attack bomber crews and thirteen carrier bombers were chosen from among us, including Ensigns Horinouchi and Kurozaki. This man Horinouchi attended high school in Taipei and holds a law degree from Tokyo University. His family still lives in Formosa, and it has been three years since he last saw his parents. Come to think of it, I remember how he always looked ill at ease and lonely each time we were allowed visitors during our seaman and student reserve days. Anyway, for him, the path to the other world, the path he is now about to follow, will be the familiar route he always used to take on visits back to Formosa. And thus he makes his first "homeward" journey in three long years. Horinouchi related these thoughts to us, softly, and with deep feeling, before setting out.

We learned today that the Koiso Cabinet has resigned en masse. That incompetent, do-nothing government collapsed in a dither without achieving anything. What's more, they had the nerve to say things like, "We resign with high hopes for the new cabinet," or "The war hasn't gone according to our wishes." What are they thinking? Is anything at all, given the present circumstances, going "according to our wishes"? For the men at the front, a single mistake means death. How is it acceptable for the prime minister simply to resign, alive, all the while publicly admitting that his deficient policies steered the nation into this crisis? Not that I mind being rid of him, of course. But he is far too selfish and irresponsible, both in his thinking and in his behavior. I can't begin to express my sorrow for the young men who fell victim to the incompetence of these politicians, young men whose deaths they rendered pointless.

Lieutenant Fujii cursed the Naval Academy graduates, egotistical men who always scurry to cover their own asses, but I hear that once he went into the battle, he fought honorably. He was making a run at a battleship when a Grumman intercepted him. He turned and, for an hour and a half, fought tenaciously to escape, until at last he was able again to home in on another battleship. He made three tries at it before plunging instead into an enemy carrier. Our fellow pilot Nagasawa radioed back with details as, one by one, the young trainees struck their targets, spitting fire. Finally he simply said, "Now I will go," and flung himself straight into a battleship. Not one of these pilots was a so-called "career" military man. I can't help comparing them, as they die, to General Koiso and his lot, and the comparison fills me with indignation.

In the early evening, six men who hadn't flown since mid-March, including Togawa, Watanabe, and Shibuya, were suddenly called out. They are to be incorporated into a special attack force at another base. They set out overland a scant twenty minutes after being asked, "Are you ready?" and only five minutes after the decision itself had been finalized. They left the base quite literally "without a moment's delay."

At around three o'clock in the morning a handful of B-29s penetrated our airspace. I assume they were coming in low, as I heard an oppressive whine. We were simply too sleepy, though. And none of us bothered to get out of bed, taking solace in the idea that, anyway, we were all in the same boat.

Carrier bombers embarked on a special attack mission at eight twenty this morning. They are to take off from Kushira at around one in the afternoon, and, together with some carrier attack bombers, dive into enemy ships. And with this, the carrier bomber ensigns serving their duty-under-instruction are all gone. As for the carrier attack bombers, there is not a single flight-worthy aircraft left at Usa Air Station. It looks like I have survived again. I don't say I am glad or happy, but still, I can't help experiencing a certain emotion.

Finally it is a nice spring day again today. The sky is hazy but cloudless. The cherry blossoms have begun to fall at last, as fresh green leaves appear to take their places. I don't know if it's a characteristic of the cherry trees in Kyushu, but they have certainly been in bloom for a long period of time. The feeling of the wind on my skin reminds me of the evenings along the canal in Kyoto in May or June. Trifoliate oranges and lily magnolias. Broad beans, rapes, daikon radishes, lotus flowers, violets. Gazing at the fields, and at the flowers that cover them, makes me feel keenly how alive I am.

After seeing off the carrier bomber squadron, we moved, the cadets to the shelter on the other side of the Yakkan River, and we to the girls' school. As we left the barracks, I noticed Fujikura's military cap where it lay on a shelf, covered with dust. Obviously we had forgotten to give it to his family. We are all excited to be bunking in the large room of a school building, as if we were at a training camp. We laid tatami mats out on the floor, put up some shelves, organized our trunks and flight jackets, and hung up a calendar. We even arranged some flowers, exercising a great deal of organizational spirit. A forty-tatami room for fifty men. What with all our gear cluttering up the space, three men will have to share two tatami mats when we sleep.

Rumor has it that Usa Air Station will be disbanded as of May 1. We'll be dispersed to bases all around the country. Some of us may undergo training in ground combat, though, again, probably as a part of a special attack force. It doesn't really matter, but still I want to die in the sky, if possible. It seems our recent military gains are far too small, given the number of radio messages that come into the base. What's more, considering what we *do* hear, the enemy force doesn't seem to be at all weakened. Their landing force has advanced up to four kilometers on Shuri. Why is this happening? When special attack aircraft target a battleship or an aircraft carrier and shift into position for a charge, they send out a coded message such as "I will now attack." Some speculate that many of the planes are downed by antiaircraft fire between the time they send this message and the time they actually reach the target, and that's why the results are disappointing. I don't know what to think. It just makes me anxious.

From one of the classrooms echoed the chorus of "Der Leiermann."

We were raided twice by B-29s.

I was assistant officer of the day today. At one point I left the OD's room and stepped into the gun room to have breakfast. The moment my chopsticks touched the rice bowl the desk heaved upwards and thrashed me in the face. Before I knew it, I was crawling on the floor amid the clay debris of the walls. As I made my way out of the room, I noticed a man off to my side, already dead. I still don't know who it was.

We had received word early on that some B-29s had left their base in the Marianas, but the Kure Naval District stood down to Defense Condition 2 at around eight twenty, and, following suit, our base issued the "all clear." So we were taken by surprise. Ten B-29s attacked at eight thirty, and twelve more came in at eight forty-five, dropping one bomb right in front of the OD's room, and another onto the telegraph room next to it. If I hadn't left the OD's room to have breakfast, I would, to say the very least, have been seriously injured. During the second raid, the sentry at the gate, a veteran in his mid-forties, lost his head. He kept running around and screaming, neglecting to take shelter. We had to punch him to get him to lie down on the ground. My eardrums had had it, and for a while I lived in a mute world. It was a trifling raid, but it inflicted enormous casualties, and the death toll neared two hundred. That figure includes seven carrier attack bomber students and two carrier bomber students. It was unfortunate that many of the men were gathered at the breakfast table at the time of bombing, since the alarm had been called off. The biggest mistake was that Usa Air Station had been under the jurisdiction of Kure Naval Station, when it should naturally have been under Sasebo.

A body without a head, an arm without a body, and what looked like a lump of guts. In addition, agonizing howls from the medical ward, as surgeons amputate legs without anesthetic.

Time bombs scattered about the airfield have put it totally out of commission. We have difficulty communicating orders, and make little progress recovering bodies. I go out with a pail to pick up stray hands, or legs with the shoes still on. A brain bisected by shards from a bomb looks like a cross section taken along a fault line. As was the case with Fujikura, men who die from injuries like this shed very little blood.

Ensign Makita's sister happened by for a visit this afternoon, the very day when he was severely injured and now lay in critical condition. She was granted special permission to see him, though he didn't acknowledge her. She insisted on staying to look after her brother, but the request was denied. She left the base, her eyes red, saying she would remain in Beppu to monitor his condition. It's strange how family members some- times pay a visit just after a man is killed in action, or on the day he is to make his sortie.

The girls' school we were using as barracks was also struck by firebombs and burned to the ground. I lost my shoes, but my clothing was saved. I'm truly sorry for the girls. I haven't eaten anything since morning, except for one rice ball, at around two in the afternoon. I have been too agitated all day to feel any hunger. Dinner was hardtack, which I soon tired of. Hardtack makes me parched as all hell.

Slept in a bunker along the Yakkan River. Incessant groans during the night. Then I heard men talking nearby, "It's heavy," "Yeah, it sure is," as they carried away a victim who had just died.

Each division dug a pit today to burn the one hundred fifty bodies we've so far managed to recover. Lieutenant Ioka's wife attended the cremation, their newborn baby in her arms. Come to think of it, I can't count anymore just how many bodies we've buried along this riverside.

In the afternoon, we began repairing the airfield. Time bombs still explode now and then, making the work quite dangerous. The flames of the funeral pyres died down in the early evening, but the bodies hadn't yet been consumed. Ensign Kado's midsection still remained pretty much intact. It might have bled if you poked it with a stick. Now I can watch and listen as the flesh of my comrades is seared on scorched galvanized sheet metal, without so much as a shudder. I guess I've grown extremely insensitive to death. As for my own life, however, I still seem to possess a strong instinct to protect that. I flee, like a streak of lightning, before I even know it. I have no clue as to what may happen when I dive into my target. But anyway I have no attachment to personal belongings, to clothing or any other property. I do regret just a little, though, that I loaned Mokichi's *Winter Clouds* to T. It burned up, along with the chest of drawers he kept it in.

After the sun set, we went to the farmer's house on top of the hill to use their bath. I looked at the beautiful roses in their yard as I waited my turn. A big moon showed itself on the way back.

Operation Kikusui, Number 4, has begun. Today, our country mounted a full-scale attack on Okinawa. As far as Usa Air Station is concerned, however, the whole thing is someone else's affair, and no wonder: we don't have any airplanes. Questionable rumors of our transfer are still making the rounds. The story goes that the carrier attack bomber division will be transferred either to Hyakuri-hara, in Ibaraki Prefecture, or else to Chitose, in Hokkaido.

An enemy task force of fourteen aircraft carriers has been sighted at Okinawa. All I can do is pray for the country. We live in the cave now, a dark, smelly, dank existence. Our clothes get damp within a day's time, and it is quite chilly at night. It seems I caught a cold, as my temperature approached thirty-nine degrees. I received a blow on the chin for looking so languid. I don't know what to think about hitting someone simply because he has a fever. But no matter. We will endure it, come what may. We fashioned a canvas canopy to prevent the dirt from falling down on us, and to pretty the place up a bit we displayed some dolls and neatly spread out the blankets that escaped the fire. But the lights are hardly on at all throughout the day.

The riverside is very pleasant in the morning. I tread across the wet sand to wash my face, and notice the tracks of a wagtail, or some other little bird, patterning the beach. Small translucent fish cling to the riverbed under the currents that gently roll in from the sea. When I rinse my mouth, the water clouds up from the toothpaste, obscuring them. Before long, Baku, the dog the carrier bomber group keeps, turns up from somewhere and hangs around, wagging its tail. Such is my morning routine. Baku is a shaggy mutt. Recently, she gave birth to puppies, which are so adorable I don't know what to say. We attack bomber crews plan to adopt one of them, but we have to wait a little while longer, until they are weaned.

I guess I'm lucky to have survived this long, but the thought of it gives me a pang. We form the backbone of this base. We are the most senior aircrews under the commander now, with the exception of a few recon men from the 13th Class. More than two-thirds of the former 13th Class students have been killed at the front. Now the fate of the nation entirely depends on how *we* die.

We need more fuel and aircraft.

MAY 3

We were granted an excursion for the first time in forty-nine days. I've recovered from my cold. I stopped by a number of places, the Kajiya Inn in Kamegawa, the bookstore, Senbiki-ya, and the barbershop in Beppu. Wherever I went, everybody was stunned, as if I'd returned from Hell or something. I got a hearty welcome. The beer was good, as were the summer oranges, and the Spanish mackerel sashimi was delicious.

"How is Ensign Fujikura?"

"How about Mr. Sakai?"

Each time I was asked these questions, I had to tell the story again of how their lives had ended. In reply, some could say nothing more than "Right. . .", their eyes brimming with tears.

"I really don't want any more of you to die," one woman said. "Isn't there any way at all to end this war?" Actually, this was the proprietress of the barbershop. I was at a loss as to what to say to her.

"That's just not how it works," I said cheerfully, making a perfunctory reply. "This is only the beginning."

The era when the special attack force was sanctified is over with. Nobody in the navy considers it "special" now. Only the newspapers keep deifying it, vulgarly, habitually. And now that the mystique has been dispelled, we all feel freer to express our anguish as ordinary men. I guess this means that, emotionally anyway, we feel a bit more natural, and our minds are more at ease. However, when his time comes, every crewman departs wearing a lovely, graceful expression. Probably I will, too, and yet when I hear words like those of the barber, I'm suddenly overcome with longing for the "free" world again, and I start thinking, say, about my mother.

After being confined to base for so long, I enjoyed the excursion immensely, but by the time the sun went down and I headed back, I was seized with an indescribable loneliness, as always at the end of an outing. A swarm of river crabs was crawling out of a cliffside onto the street. As I approached, they watched me warily, bodies half withdrawn back into their holes. Then I went after the ones on the street, and they scurried away angrily, red claws raised. I loitered there for a while, goofing around with the crabs. I was lonesome.

At last, Germany has surrendered. The sword is broken, the quiver is empty. The Red Army has virtually seized Berlin. Hamburg Radio, the only station still in German hands, has announced that Hitler died on the afternoon of May 1. Admiral Doenitz has been appointed supreme commander of the armed forces, but I guess his duty will essentially be to negotiate the terms of surrender. I also hear that Mussolini was captured and killed, his body exposed in a square in Milan.

MAY 7

Some forty B-29s assaulted the base this morning, badly damaging the apron. There weren't many casualties, as we had been on full alert, but the time bombs prevent us from going out. They blow up now and then, like land mines, kicking a cloud of dust more than a hundred meters into the air. Judging from this, the enemy's bombs must be more powerful than our 800 kg No.80s. The fierce blasts even reach our cave, five hundred meters from the airfield.

A group of army planes called the "Toryu" intercepted the enemy, achieving some results. One charged into a B-29, taking it down on Mt. Hachimen. A few enemy fliers bailed out in parachutes, and Ensign Nikaido and I set out to capture them. We combed the hill with the help of a civil defense unit and managed to seize two men toward evening. They emerged with their hands up, looking carefree. They were both twenty-two, and roughly correspond to trainees in our country, or so it appears. One is a Sergeant Romance, and I forgot the name of the other. Sgt. Romance was a gunner on the port side. When he saw a Japanese fighter closing in from the left, he instinctively judged that it would smash into the plane, and he bailed out in a panic. He actually had the nerve to say that he was hungry, and as we passed through Nakatsu, he waved his hands, smiling at the crowd that had gathered out of curiosity. I don't know if I should properly call him ingenuous or hateful. Either way, it's astonishing to see how utterly his temperament differs from ours. When showered with blows, he frowns a bit, but then he looks as if nothing at all had happened. Seeing as how we had suffered such heavy casualties from the bombings, some among us were in an uproar, and insisted that we rough the Americans up. However, we received strict orders as to the handling of the prisoners. As for Romance and his comrade, they seem to have no fear at all for their safety. Apparently, they assume U.S. forces will rescue them soon enough.

Today, word came that we'll be transferred to Hyakuri-hara. Each is to board the train at his convenience and leave here on the 11th. Usa Naval Air Station will be disbanded.

At sunset, the naval ensign was lowered. We saluted in the cave, from a distance. All the buildings on the base are in ruins. Watching the flag slowly go down for the last time in the tranquil evening sun, I felt deep emotion. Usa was severe, but all the more rewarding for it. With Beppu nearby, we were blessed with a hot spring and plentiful food. Also, we sent off so many of our friends from this place. They will never come back.

Hyakuri-hara is situated in the most out-of-the-way place in Ibaraki Prefecture. There isn't a house for twelve kilometers in any direction, I hear. It's also a long way to the nearest railway station. Enjoyable outings will be pretty much out of the question.

On May 11, as the "all clear" was issued, we left Usa Naval Air Station in the rain and took the northbound train that leaves Yanagiga-ura at 1400. Romance and his friend stayed behind in the hands of the remaining force and should be sent to some camp or other before long. Our seats were in a second-class car. It was pleasant, not at all like a troop train. Each man received a bottle of wine, three bags of crackers, and a ration of flight food. I saved mine for later, as I wanted to eat it at my home in Osaka. The train was seven hours late by the time it arrived in Osaka. I got a close look at the bombed-out sites there and at Kobe. It was horrible. All of a sudden, images of San Francisco, Chicago, and New York came to mind—those self-satisfied American cities, secure in their stone-built prosperity and without so much as a scratch to mar them. And I thought, never again can I persuade myself that we might win this war. We simply have to fight and fight and fight, all the way down until we meet our end.

Nobody was at the station for me. I later learned that my father and uncle had waited from nine in the morning till five in the afternoon, until they finally got tired and went home, just before the train pulled in.

I left the station and found the city of Osaka rough and unkind, overcome with war-weariness. Wherever I went, I met cold looks and sulking faces. Not that I want them to show any special courtesy just because I'm a navy pilot, but I didn't see even the slightest sign of a willingness to bear a part. What a change since I left here in my school uniform one and a half years ago in a rain of hurrahs! On the tram, I came across an old bird in a workman's waistcoat and puttees, dangling a duffel bag.

"What the hell do they think they'll do now?" he said, addressing me point-blank. "Damn stupid of them to start such a hopeless war!" I struggled so hard to resist the temptation to turn on him that I couldn't enjoy the old familiar Osaka dialect.

The pain, however, didn't last long. Once I made my way to our old home, which had escaped the fires, it was good to be with my father, good to be with my mother. The place was suffused with the nostalgic scent of home, and I found it hard to leave again. That night, I chatted over drinks amid the familiar faces of my father's three brothers, and of K. and M., who are staying with my family, until half past two in the morning.

On the 13th, I dropped in on a few neighbors and then left home at eleven. My mother hadn't gotten a wink of sleep, and neither, by the looks of it, had my father. I was the only one who had had a good, sound sleep. At Otake Naval Barracks, at Himeji Station, and in Beppu—so often have I parted with my father, each time supposing it would be the last I ever saw of him, and yet today I again had the good fortune to be escorted to Osaka Station by him. Looking at the devastated landscape along the Yodo River as the train sped across it made me feel broken-hearted. Tears rose in my eyes.

I broke my journey at Kyoto and headed straight for Kyoto University. It was very careless of me, though, to have forgotten that it was Sunday. I couldn't find anyone, and I didn't have time to make it out to Professor E.'s house. I left Kyoto in haste on the 1645 train. What a shame.

It was past five the next morning by the time I arrived in Tokyo. At Ueno Station, I boarded the 1403 train on the Joban Line to go to Ishioka, and there I changed to a light railway that took me to Ogawa. I arrived at Hyakuri-hara at close to seven in the evening. The base is eight kilometers from Ogawa, and there is no public transportation between the town and the base. Since I arrived here, I have been living like a drone, day after day. Training flights start tomorrow. Twenty-eight pilots have been chosen.

MAY 26

Tokyo has suffered an extensive raid again last night. Some two hundred fifty B-29s carried out indiscriminate attacks against the urban districts from ten thirty to two thirty. The uptown area seems particularly to have suffered.

Standing outside at Hyakuri-hara, I could see balls of fire floating in the skies over Tokyo. These were B-29s that had been shot. They don't go down easily, even when engulfed in flame. They seemed to be sucking up the red, yellow, and green tracer bullets coming at them from every direction. Plunging down in flames, and drawing a straight line, like a meteor, was a Japanese fighter. It was all a gorgeous feast of celestial fire. Our side reportedly shot down twenty-seven B-29s during the raid the night before last, and forty-seven more last night. It might be the usual over-reporting, but it doesn't seem incredible, either.

I decided to go to Tokyo and got dressed at three o'clock instead of going to bed. I walked the eight kilometers to Ogawa, and took the first light railway train to Ishioka. I managed to reach Ueno Station only to find that, for the most part, transportation was at a standstill in Tokyo. I had intended to drop in at K.'s place, but there were no trains running to Meguro. I had no choice but to turn back. I got off at Tsuchiura and spent the night at the Officers' Mess. Tsuchiura made me a little nostalgic, but I was too exhausted to drop in anywhere.

When I returned to base, I learned that the Army's Giretsu Airborne Unit had landed at the north and central airfields on Okinawa. They went on a rampage, achieving significant military results. Still, I have a vague feeling that Okinawa is nearing its last stage. Evidently, Operation Kikusui came to nothing in the end.

MAY 30

It's my twenty-fifth birthday.

Training flights keep us occupied every day. Around here, when the cold, damp northeastern winds start to blow in the evening, a thick fog streams in from the sea. If I look at the broad ocean from the air, I can watch as the dense fog bank creeps in over the surface of the water, moving to the southwest, in handfuls. The altitude of the fog is less than one hundred fifty meters, and eventually it engulfs the airfield, reducing visibility to ten meters or less. And then abruptly, it starts to clear away in places, as if a curtain were being raised. But the evening sun shines full on my plane, fog or no fog, and as I fly freely over the drifting clouds, or over the banks of fog, I always experience anew the strange fascination of riding through the sky. It delights me. Still, I guess it's inevitable now that the decisive battle will be fought on mainland Japan. Assuming that the nearby Kashima Sea and Kuju-kuri Beach are among the most imperiled sites (*these* are certainly not "somebody else's affair"), I look carefully down at the shoreline, hoping to spot some new defense works, each time I fly. But I see nothing of the sort. What do they intend to do?

The raids against the Tokyo-Yokohama district have rapidly intensified. Five hundred B-29s and one hundred P-51s flew over at around nine o'clock yesterday morning, for the most part concentrating their attack on Yokohama. This was the first time that their fighters and bombers flew over together in droves, and in broad daylight, too. Even the skies over Hyakuri-hara darkened during the attack, as if blanketed in thick clouds, so that some of the men said, "Is it going to rain?"

We had a ration of strawberries in the evening. Red, glossy, and sweet. Each time I see a rabbit-ear iris or eat strawberries, I appreciate the occasion deeply. I take it as the last blessing of the season.

JUNE 9

Hyakuri-hara Air Station is responsible for patrolling a fan-shaped area of the sea to the east of Inubo-zaki and the Onahama line. Every day, reconnaissance crews set out to scour this zone. Each plane departs from the pivot of the fan, proceeds along its individually designated line (constituting, say, one rib of the fan), and then traces a path back down the adjacent line in a route that forms a long isosceles triangle. Along some of these lines, however, one cannot fly without being shot down, or so it's believed, anyway, almost like myth. There might be a logical reason behind this, such as that the regular incursions of enemy fighters cross our patrol lines there at a slight angle, but whatever the case, we simply can't avoid patrolling these routes. And they are always assigned to former student reservists, never to an officer from the Naval Academy.

I don't know what will ultimately be written about the Imperial Navy, or about the education men receive at the Naval Academy, with its (supposed) spirit of patriotic self-sacrifice. I have no idea what the future will say about any of this. But how often the precept "A superior officer's order is implicitly the order of the Emperor himself" is used, conveniently, to provide cover for essentially selfish acts! And the problem is not confined to naval air stations like Hyakuri, I should think.

JUNE 14

According to the commanding officer, we have lost radio contact with Okinawa. It's raining again today. The rainy season seems to have arrived.

In the afternoon, we had a lecture on special attack maneuvers. I'm constantly sleepy. Nowadays, enemy planes might be flying in overhead all day long, but still, I'm simply sleepy.

While our bodies are overcome with fatigue, our minds are somehow eager, and a pseudo-elegant aestheticism is now in fashion at this base. Poetry readings, flower arranging, what have you. The buckwheat is in bloom, the peony also. As have many others, I arranged, free-style, a large bouquet of Chinese peonies, together with sprigs of azalea, in a basin I had on hand. Complacently, I flatter myself that the result looks pretty good. In a farmer's house I saw some silkworms feeding on mulberry leaves, making their faint noises, and it brought back distant, sweet memories of my boyhood, when I myself raised a few silkworms in a box, with holes pierced in it. It feels as if I were looking back at my life in its closing years.

The pseudo-elegance continues. I look out for various flowers, and learn the names of them. Buckwheat, tomato, thistle, coreopsis, asthmaweed, red smartweed, wild rose, water lily, sago palm, Reeve's meadowsweet, gladiola, pomegranate (I remember seeing this in Minamata last year, a red, stiff-looking flower), zinnia, marguerite (white petals with a yellow center), cornflower (the German national flower), fringed pink, pink, sacred bamboo, kabotcha, cucumber, eggplant, dahlia, evening primrose, chestnut, and rose moss.

And there are more. Some off-season flowers, too. Common dayflower, bindweed, dokudami, hydrangea, garden balsam, stone leek, tiger lily, daikon, garden stonecrop, castorbean, and Indian strawberry.

We flew in formation over Lake Kasumiga-ura. I saw a thin cloud drifting two hundred meters above the surface of the lake, in a strip some thirty meters wide.

I hear that various kinds of "special attack" aircraft are now being tested. The "Kikka" is said to be particularly promising. This is a jet-propelled, twin-engine aircraft that boasts a cruising speed of three hundred knots. But then again, I remember that Germany was herself hardly lacking in prototype weapons, and she was defeated just before any of them went into use.

A new special attack force has been organized. I'm first on the list. I feel suddenly awake. I move at once to Kisarazu, in Chiba Prefecture. Looks like it's my turn to make a sortie.

They held a send-off party for me. No sake. We sang together and made believe we were drunk. I leave here tomorrow. I will know all once I arrive.

Farewell note 1.
To my parents.
Jiro
July 9, Showa 20 (1945)
At Kisarazu Naval Air Station

I haven't written you for a while. I moved to this area hastily at the end of June. The enemy task force left Saipan, and its whereabouts have been unknown for the last two or three days. We think it's highly probable that they will invade the mainland this morning, so we have been on standby since four o'clock. I'm writing this note beside my plane. As soon as we locate the task force, I will set out as part of a special attack force.

I am immensely grateful for the twenty-five years of care and love that you have given me. I appreciate what you must be feeling, but I truly hope that you are assured I go in peace and am content with my mission; and also that you will not grieve too much about my fate.

Various things have set me to brooding, but last night I had a good dinner and slept deeply. When the time comes, I believe I really can embark with a light heart, just as so many of my friends have, so please don't be troubled about me.

May you be in good health whatever comes, that is all I earnestly pray for.

There is nothing I must ask you to take care of after I'm gone. No financial problems, no relationships that might need sorting out. Tend to my books as you see fit. There is this person, by the way: Miss Fukiko Fukai, of Minamata, Kumamoto Prefecture. She was very kind to us when we were in training at Izumi. I might have mentioned her to you if I had lived. It is not necessary, though, for you to contact the Fukais, since Fukiko knows nothing of my feelings for her, and since we have not corresponded with each other. I just wanted to tell you about her, as she might come to my mind, together with images of you two, as I crash into my target.

It is now half past eight. Excuse my scribbled note. So long.

Farewell note 2.
To Kashima.

The clouds are my tomb.
Setting sun, grace my epitaph.

My dear old friend, how are you faring? Remember our time in Kyoto, when we studied and had such fun together. We hashed it all out over cups of sake. Those were the good hours, the precious hours. Oh—Otsu, Yamashina, the seaweed offshore at the town of Nabari, the shallows of the Furukawa River. Even after we joined the navy, fate saw to it that we lived under the same roof, never failing to accompany each other. My friend, have you ever thought about that? Close as we were, we seldom had a quiet, heart-to-heart talk. There may be no end to regret, once I am gone, but I hope this letter will do, anyway, as a reminder of something.

My friend, keep yourself well.

Morning, July 9th

Jiro Yoshino

Letter by Kashima

October, Showa 20 (1945)
Parents of Jiro Yoshino
Takebuchi, Yao-cho
Naka Kawachi-gun, Osaka

I can only imagine how lonely and inconvenient life must be at your evacuation camp. Already two months have passed since we lost the war, and obscure feelings have me utterly in their grip. After being demobilized, I left my hometown and set out on an aimless, wandering journey with the help of a small sum of money, and of some friends and acquaintances. I do intend to return to the campus in Kyoto, but I don't feel like doing it just yet. I lost every one of the three friends who joined the navy with me in the middle of our academic pursuits. The shock is too great for me.

As for the final hours of your son's life, I do not know the from the stories of his comrades who were stationed at the same base, once the world calms down. So far, I have checked closely the back-issues of newspapers, and the like, from the period, but I find no articles that appear to concern your son's mission. I noticed, however, that on the morning of July 10, a U.S. task force approached mainland Japan, and that a total of more than eight hundred planes raided airfields in the Kanto district in several waves. Judging from the date of the farewell note I received from your son, I would say that he probably embarked on a special attack mission that day, and that he dived into a U.S. aircraft carrier at sea to the east of Japan. I do not know why you have not received an official report from the navy. Possibly it was mislaid in the confusion of defeat. At any rate, it is utterly inexcusable, and I am very sorry for that.

I am staying in a town called Ubara, on the eastern coast of Chiba Prefecture. In any case, I believe your son's body rests somewhere far from this shore. I am certain that he reposes in peace at the horizon, where ocean and sky meet, with the sea for his grave, and his epitaph written in the clouds. It is a beautiful shoreline, with its many twists and turns, and its sheer cliff rising. Japanese silverleaves grow thick on the cliffside, producing their yellow flowers. The coastline here probably touches on the arc of the great circling route to America, as I often see what look like large American steamers sail by offshore. A storm seems to be at hand. The clouds are disturbed and the water is troubled, though the sun occasionally appears.

I enclose a clumsy poem that I wrote along this shore, to be placed by his picture. I will certainly visit you when I get back to Kyoto, sometime in the future, and talk with you at length.

With kindest personal regards.

"A Visit to the Grave"
—*Dedicated to the late Jiro Yoshino*

Today I climbed
This headland mountain
Where the southern winds blow in.
And I bowed deeply at your grave,
You who shall never come back.

The ocean;
The cradle of the deep;
Your grave.
Toward me, under blue-tinted clouds that
    seethe and break,
How the vast blue currents heave!

On that day
The struggle swallowed you up.
And now that peace has come
A thousand waves caress you,
And your epitaph gleams in the clouds.

Ah, that epitaph:
It quickens again
The old days, with a sweet pang,

The days we talked together over cups of sake,
The good hours, the precious hours.

Southern winds blow in
From the sea,
Agitating the grass at my feet
And my heart also.
Facing the ocean, I call your name, helpless.